A Candlelight Ecstasy Romance®

"YOU LISTEN TO ME, BECAUSE I MEAN EVERY WORD I'M ABOUT TO SAY!" ANNABEL RAGED.

"I don't know why you're here, but whatever the reason, you will not upset my life a second time, nor will you hurt the people I love. I'm not the meek little innocent that you seduced eleven years ago—"

"What are you, Annabel?" Luke cut in.

"At peace," she told him. "I have my future all mapped out. I know exactly where I'm going, and I don't intend to let anyone stop me, not now!"

"Well, I hate to throw a wrench in your plans, but I'm suddenly wondering why I ever let you go," Luke said, his hand snaking around her waist.

CANDLELIGHT ECSTASY CLASSIC ROMANCES

CANDLELIGHT ECSTASY ROMANCES®

AN INVITATION TO LOVE

Kathy Orr

A CANDLELIGHT ECSTASY ROMANCE®

Published by
Dell Publishing Co., Inc.
1 Dag Hammarskjold Plaza
New York, New York 10017

ISBN: 0-440-14127-3

Printed in the United States of America

August 1987

10 9 8 7 6 5 4 3 2 1

WFH

To Our Readers:

We have been delighted with your enthusiastic response to Candlelight Ecstasy Romances®, and we thank you for the interest you have shown in this exciting series.

In the upcoming months we will continue to present the distinctive sensuous love stories you have come to expect only from Ecstasy. We look forward to bringing you many more books from your favorite authors and also the very finest work from new authors of contemporary romantic fiction.

As always, we are striving to present the unique, absorbing love stories that you enjoy most—books that are more than ordinary romance. Your suggestions and comments are always welcome. Please write to us at the address below.

Sincerely,

The Editors
Candlelight Romances
1 Dag Hammarskjold Plaza
New York, New York 10017

AN INVITATION TO LOVE

CHAPTER ONE

The handwriting caught his attention immediately. Not too much correspondence crossed his desk marked *Very Confidential* in carefully formed script which indicated that the writer was of tender years. Ignoring the other mail, none of which, he was sure, would stir him to anything other than borderline indifference, he drew the ivory envelope toward him.

Not the average dime-store stationery, he acknowledged, the linen texture pleasantly abrasive against his fingertips. Then he noticed the Vancouver postmark and something stirred uneasily in the undiscovered layers of his mind. For a moment, he tested the point of the brass letter opener against the ball of his thumb, insanely tempted to toss the letter, unread, into the wastebasket. But boredom was an insidious disease. It spurred a man into all kinds of impulses he might later come to regret.

So he slit the envelope cleanly against the fold and the two sheets of notepaper inside spilled all their revelations and secrets onto his desk. And the even tenor of Luke Barrington's life, the predictability of which he'd found stifling for some time, came to a sudden halt. Curiosity erupted inside him with a vigor that even he, jaded as he felt himself to be, recognized

9

as exhilaration. "Well, I'll be damned," he said softly, after a third, intent reading.

"You actually mailed it?" Sybil raised reproachful brows at her granddaughter. "Without letting me read it first?"

Pandora came as close to blushing as was possible for a ten-year-old normally possessed of more poise than most women of thirty. "Grandmother, this is between a daughter and—" She caught sight of Annabel in the doorway and flashed her a guilty look before gathering her wits into their customary order. "Hi, Mom. We didn't know you were back already. Does it fit?"

"Well enough. What were you talking about?"

"Well enough? Annabel, you can't settle for that!" Sybil was aghast.

"Invitations," Pandora improvised hurriedly. "We were talking about invitations—about one we forgot to mail."

"So why would you want to read it first, Mother?" Annabel persisted. "What's to read on an engraved invitation that you don't already know about?"

"Never mind the invitations." Agitated, Sybil rose from the sofa by the open french doors and paced to the fireplace. "We're talking about your wedding dress, Annabel. 'Well enough' won't do."

"I'm losing weight." Annabel shrugged indifferently, then focused her attention on her ten-year-old daughter. "Why do I feel as though you're trying to bamboozle me, Pandora?"

"I don't know, Mommy." Pandora regarded her out of large, guileless eyes. "Maybe it's your imagination,

10

or wedding nerves. Maybe you're not as calm as you think."

Annabel remained near the doorway, leaning lightly against the silk-paneled wall. "What I think," she said, her gaze narrowing suspiciously, "is that the last time you called me 'Mommy,' without having something devious in the works, was when you decided you were adopted and about to be sent back to the orphanage. Don't make those big gray eyes at me, Pandora. I wasn't born yesterday."

"Annabel, my treasure!" Sybil swooped down on her daughter and enveloped her in a scented hug. "You may not have been born yesterday, but you're naïve as a baby. Don't be quizzing the child this way. A bridesmaid's permitted to have a few secrets, and it's a bride's duty to be suitably surprised when they're revealed. Would you like something? Tea, perhaps, or lemonade with mint?"

Annabel detached herself from her mother and regarded her family with undimmed mistrust. "Vodka," she declared. "With tonic. I've a gut feeling I'm going to need it." She crossed to the sofa, sank against the down-filled cushions, and stretched her legs. "Bring me up to date on the latest arrangements."

"Well . . ." Sybil, busily exchanging conspiratorial glances with Pandora, almost tripped over Annabel's feet. "Good grief, don't tell me you went for a fitting in those shoes?"

"Why not?" Annabel yawned, and laced her fingers through her hair so that it sprang in disobedient curls all over her head. "What would you like me to wear to the hospital, Mother, ballet slippers? These are perfectly good shoes."

"They are not shoes," Sybil informed her scorn-

11

fully. "They're World War One trench-hoppers, and I fail to see the need for them. You're teaching impressionable young girls to be ministering angels, for heaven's sake, not foot soldiers."

"Stop trying to change the subject, Mother. What's been going on around here?"

"Oh . . ." Sybil fluttered her hands, geranium-red nails flashing. ". . . we're so organized, it's disgusting. People start arriving tomorrow and we're having the reception—nothing formal, just cocktails and hors d'oeuvres—for Jeremy's parents, the night after. This week's busy, but next week's impossible. The house will be bursting at the seams with guests coming from all over, but I expect—"

"None of this is news, Mother. Tell me what it is you've done that's making you babble, and has Pandora eyeing you as if she's afraid you're about to let a two-headed cat out of the bag."

Sybil snapped her jaw shut, just briefly, and cast an affronted glare at her daughter. "Well, *somebody* has to be nervous, and you're clearly above anything so conventional. If it's vodka you're pouring, I'll have one, too."

"You're sounding very Irish, Mother, and that, all by itself, is enough to make me nervous."

Sybil watched as Annabel unlaced her shoes and eased them from her narrow, elegant feet. "At the very least," Sybil persisted, her gaze following her daughter as she rose from the couch and made her unhurried way to the cocktail bar, "you could succumb to a bit of excitement. All this tranquillity in a bride just two weeks short of the altar is offensive."

"That's because it's a marriage of convenience," Pandora piped up, managing to dispel her mother's composure and reduce her grandmother to gasping seizures of horror.

The ice sprang from the tongs Annabel held poised above a glass, clattered noisily over the polished surface of the table, then slid to the carpet. And in the living room of the house in which Annabel had lived since her birth thirty years before, three generations of Pryce women looked anywhere but at each other as the enormity of Pandora's ten-year-old wisdom took its effect.

Sybil pretended to recover first. "The child," she pronounced, somewhat asthmatically to Annabel's trained ear, "watches altogether too much TV. Pandora, my lamb, tell your mother—"

"Where you first heard that expression," Annabel cut in. "And please don't blame it on 'Sesame Street.'"

Pandora, the least perturbed of them all, surveyed her mother pityingly through unclouded eyes. "Of course not. More likely 'All My Children,' but I think I read about it somewhere, and it means two people getting married because it's . . . well, convenient. You know what I mean, Mommy? Actually, in all the best shows, they have the other kind—the sort where people get married because they can't stand not to."

"Out of the mouths of babes," Sybil muttered and, at Annabel's sharply suspicious glance, occupied herself rearranging a vase of flowers.

"What was that, Mother?"

"Aphids," Sybil improvised. "The roses have aphids. Remind me to tell Harry in the morning."

"I will, Mother, but for now, let's examine the reason for Pandora making such an extraordinary—not to mention adult—observation." Annabel directed her

13

gaze equally between her mother and her daughter, taking peripheral note that Sybil's discombobulation grew in direct proportion to Pandora's mutinous silence. *"I have all evening, ladies. And all night, if necessary." So saying, she settled herself against the edge of the library table, leaning back on her hands, her hips resting against the pale, polished oak. "Which one of you would like to begin?"

"Oh . . . !" Sybil clicked her tongue in defeat. "If you must know, it hasn't escaped our attention that, as a love match, this marriage between you and Jeremy leaves a lot to be desired."

"And you've discussed it together? Mother, I thought we agreed this marriage was the best possible thing for Pandora. How could you undermine what Jeremy and I are trying to provide, denigrating it this way?"

"I haven't told her anything the child couldn't figure out for herself. Mother of God, Annabel, she'd have to be blind and backward not to have seen. The *walls* have noticed."

"I thought you liked Jeremy." Bewildered, Annabel looked from one to the other.

"We do," Sybil insisted. "He's a wonderful man and we love him." She hesitated, exchanged another furtive glance with Pandora, and hurried on before she lost her nerve: "More perhaps than do you. Yet you're the one who's marrying him, Annabel."

Indignation stained Annabel's cheeks pink and left her nearly breathless. "What utter nonsense! Really, Mother, where do you get off, filling your granddaughter's head with such rubbish?"

"She didn't do that." Pandora, typically, couldn't bear to be left out of the conversation. "I thought it up

14

all by myself. There's something missing, Mommy. Even I can see that. There aren't any violins or roses or moonlight. You know what I mean?"

Thunderstruck, Annabel stared at her daughter, wondering, in her dismay, how a ten-year-old could lay bare the heart of the matter. "That," she croaked, "is terribly unfair of you, Pandora."

"But if it's the truth, my darling . . . ?" Sybil suggested.

"It's not the truth." Annabel pushed away from the table and headed across the room. "I love Jeremy," she informed her daughter in passing, and swiveling her head, flung her mother a wounded glare. "I intend to marry him," she declared, defiance sharpening the natural grace of her body into unyielding lines, "and I very much doubt there's anything you can do, Mother, to prevent that."

"That's what you think," Sybil muttered into the ice bucket.

"What?"

"Drink," the normally abstemious matriarch replied blithely. "I need a drink and so, from the looks of you, do you. Sit down, Annabel. All this stalking around is giving me the willies."

"I don't need alcohol to get me through my own wedding preparations," the bride returned loftily, choosing to ignore her previous assertion to the contrary, and made as regal an exit as could be expected of one who dangled an orthopedic nursing shoe from each hand.

Two evenings later she decided she did need some help getting through her own wedding. Clutching her champagne glass as tightly as if it were a life preserver,

15

Annabel stared across the sea of faces in the living room and fastened her horrified gaze on the man who'd materialized at the open french doors leading from the terrace.

Pure shock left her ice cold and frozen on the spot. This party was the first of a series of meticulously planned social occasions to mark her wedding, and she had allowed for no such untoward developments as this. Yet Luke Barrington had shown up, as unexpected as the plague and every bit as unwelcome.

Eleven years had wrought their handiwork on him. The dark brown hair was threaded lightly with silver and he was leaner at forty, the angled precision of jaw and cheekbone more firmly defined. But recognizable. Even had she wanted to believe her eyes had deceived her, misled by some trick of the evening's soft light, every other level of awareness in her body sprang to full alert, creating complete turmoil within her. She blinked but he was still there. Destiny, in the shape of Luke Barrington, was making an ill-timed bid to reshape the direction of her well-planned future, and she was helpless to do anything about it.

Independent of her will, her feet carried her over the carpet, narrowing the space that separated her from him with dismaying speed. The crowd, previously almost suffocating her with their attentions, melted into the dusk and left only Annabel and Luke, face to face again, recognition and knowledge humming in the air between and around them. He spoke first.

"Aloha!" he said, an undercurrent of laughter threading through his words, and raised his glass in a salute. "I bet this stuff didn't come in half-gallon jugs." And just like that, he brought the island of Maui

16

out of the mists of yesterday and back into the sharp focus of the present.

Annabel closed her lips which had fallen disconcertingly apart and left her, she was sure, looking like the village idiot. Then, when she thought she might be able to articulate a sane reply—something collected and poised and terribly clever—she opened them again. "Please don't be here," she beseeched him, and heard her words escape before she could get her mouth closed again.

He examined her from behind rimless glasses that did nothing to disguise his wonderful gray eyes—Pandora's eyes, thick-lashed and intelligent and missing nothing. "Memories," he said softly, "are so often misleading and invite nothing but disappointment, but you, Annabel, are every bit as lovely as I remembered you to be, and more."

"Please don't say things like that," she begged, his words just about stopping her heart. "Please don't talk to me. Tell me why you're here."

The ghost of a smile curled his mouth and touched his eyes with silver. "Make up your mind, Annabel. What do you want?"

"An explanation." Distracted, she glanced over her shoulder. From a distance, the civilized buzz of the party mingled with the reedy tones of a string quartet playing Mozart. Out of the corner of her eye, she saw Jeremy edging toward her. Panic dimmed her vision and involuntarily she turned back to Luke and grasped his arm. "You have no right grate-cashing," she babbled, and heard her own idiocy echo in her ears seconds before his grin burst forth. Dazzled, she lowered her eyes and sought frantically to restore her compo-

·sure. "Gate-crashing," she amended. "No one invited you. Go away."

"Fat chance." He was absolutely unmoved by her distress. "First off, I'm not gate-crashing; I was invited. And second, you owe *me* an explanation or two, and I don't propose to disappear until I get them."

Jeremy, practically at her shoulder, was accosted by a large gentleman whom Annabel didn't recognize. Seizing the opportunity to escape having to introduce the two, she reached forward and pushed Luke unceremoniously out of the french doors and back to the terrace whence he had so inconsiderately appeared.

Intercepting her harried glance, he slid a hand down her arm to capture her fingers, and dragged her after him. What a mistake that was! His touch, even in so fleeting a context, was as disturbing as his presence, and had her almost choking with nerves. How pleased her mother would be, Annabel reflected wildly, to know that the bride had shed her self-possession and was displaying all the proper signs of pre-wedding jitters. And what a pity they were brought on by the wrong man.

"Are we running away from someone, Annabel?"

"Yes," she muttered, annoyed by her body's refusal to abide by the dictates of her mind. It was purely irrational to be fluttering this way over someone whose intrusion into her life lasted only four days, and that more than a decade ago. "My fiancé."

"That was your fiancé?" Luke spun around and re-traced his steps to the french doors, hauling Annabel, willy-nilly, behind him. "Annabel, you must introduce us."

"I will not," she whispered fiercely, dragging her feet to absolutely no effect.

18

"Why not? Are you ashamed of him?" Pressing his nose to the window that flanked the doors, Luke peered through the twilight-darkened glass, slipping an arm around Annabel's shoulders as he did so.

She began to shiver even though the outside thermometer read a balmy seventy-two degrees. "Of course I'm not ashamed of him."

From inside the room, Jeremy's rather obese Aunt Marion waddled closer to the window, clearly wondering whose faces were staring through the panes so intently.

"I should hope not," Luke replied, waving affably to Marion who backed off, startled. "Especially since you've decided to appoint him custodian of my daughter. I wouldn't like to think, Annabel, that you'd be so careless as to neglect telling me I'm a father *and* hand my child into the care of a scoundrel."

"He's a surgeon," she retorted stiffly.

"But not a scoundrelly surgeon, right?" Luke's voice was pure steel underlying the silk. "Stop fidgeting, sweet thing. I know you're anxious to get back to your party, but I think I've the right to a few minutes of your time, though we can have our little talk in there with everyone listening, if that's what you'd prefer."

Annabel felt tears of frustration threatening to ruin her mascara. It was more than unfair, it was an outrage that she should be held accountable, now, for her single lapse from grace, just when she was about to crown her years of atonement with the ultimate sacrifice—

Appalled, the tears aborted with shock, she covered her mouth with her hand as though, by so doing, she could prevent her thoughts from crystallizing into truth. Marrying Jeremy—handsome, charming, responsible, and *available*—could scarcely be construed

19

a sacrifice by anyone with two neurons to rub together.

"Stubborn silences do not an answer make," Luke reprimanded her, shaking her gently, and she realized she'd missed his next question. "When were you planning to let me know I have a daughter?"

It was more than she could do to formulate an answer. He'd robbed her of the powers of rational thought with his sudden and shocking presence. In the space of ten minutes, he'd wiped out ten years of her life. Helpless to do a thing to prevent it, she watched her thirty-year-old image slide away to collapse in wrinkles around her ankles, and saw her nineteen-year-old self uncurl from its lengthy hibernation and begin to flex its cramped muscles, giddy, carefree, and hungry—though for what was something she couldn't bring herself to recognize. The whole business left her paralyzed with fear.

"Too much champagne, Annabel?" Luke's gaze, fastened on her features, took note of her pallor and her dark blue eyes huge and staring in her face.

His marked lack of sympathy, as much as the question itself, roused her to fortifying irritation. "Certainly not," she informed him shortly, and wished one of the waiters would drift by with a loaded tray. The idea of downing another glass of champagne and baptizing Luke with a third, held enormous appeal. "How did you find out about Pandora?"

"She wrote to me and spilled the beans."

Not by herself she didn't, Annabel fumed, remembering the evening a couple of days earlier when Pandora's caginess had been exceeded only by Sybil's dithery evasion. Annabel detected her mother's fine handiwork in all this. The wretches! Whatever had possessed the pair of them? They surely didn't think Luke's arrival was going to put a halt to her wedding plans? "Well, you chose a fine time to make your paternal presence felt. You've waited this long to meet your child, couldn't you have held off another month and let me enjoy my honeymoon in peace?"

The branches of an acacia tree filtered the moonlight and left her face in part shadow so that only her mouth was visible. Fascinated by the curve of her lips, he watched as she spoke and remembered with surprising intensity exactly how it had felt to kiss them, all those years ago.

Were they still as soft? he wondered, and felt a tug of desire that left him as startled as he was curious. No longer a man easily susceptible to a lovely face, he was at a loss to account for the stirrings that had taken hold of him the moment he'd stepped into the room and seen her again. In a stern effort to curb them, he reminded himself that he'd come out to the coast to verify that he had a daughter, not to renew an old acquaintance with the mother. Yet the urge to touch Annabel's face persisted.

Not moving a step closer, he raised one hand and let his fingertip ghost up the curve of her eyelashes and trace the sweep of her brow, before his palm slid down to define the shadowed contour of her jaw. "You have the cheekbones of a Romanian Gypsy," he whispered.

Trapped in a web of tension so finely wrought that it had ensnared her without warning, she found the effort of holding her eyes open and her breathing steady quite beyond her. "Russian," she managed to correct him before her throat closed completely.

He was not similarly afflicted; seemed, in fact, compelled to talk when all she wanted was for him to put his mouth to other, more intimate use, with hers. Aghast at her response, her eyes flew wide and betrayed her. A great sigh, half regret, half reproach, filled her beleaguered lungs.

At that, he fell silent, but she found him staring at her as though discovering her for the first time. His hand, warmer even than the temperate air of evening, seemed indisposed to relinquish its exploration of her jaw. "You're touching me," she accused him faintly.

"I know," he said, and would have stepped closer had the french doors not suddenly swung open and spilled the light and laughter from the party all over them.

"I tell you I saw someone!" Aunt Marion's tones, shrill with excitement, preceded her well-harnessed bosom by mere seconds. "Peering in the window at me they were. I think the Pryces've got prowlers, Jeremy."

"Most likely just guests enjoying the view," he placated her, "but if it'll make you feel better, we'll check it out."

As Jeremy, his aunt, and a following of curious guests stepped out onto the terrace, Luke gripped Annabel by the hand and with all the instincts of a night creature well able to see in the dark, darted surefootedly down the steps and into the concealing foliage of the shrubbery in the garden below.

All that anyone saw was the pale pink of Annabel's chiffon dress fluttering away into the bushes.

"Oh, Jeremy!" Marion squealed, her little fat feet rapping sharply in their high heels across the bricks. "It's more than just a prowler. He's taken Annabel. Your dear little bride's been kidnapped."

Annabel, with her hand still firmly clamped in Luke's and the billowing skirt of her pink chiffon dress

22

spread around her like a collapsed parachute, knelt in the soft moist dirt behind a giant rhododendron bush and found herself praying for deliverance, while up above, on the terrace, all hell broke loose.

CHAPTER TWO

"This is absurd!" It surely was, two grown people scrabbling around in the dirt like a pair of kids, yet she found herself whispering as though preserving the secrecy of their whereabouts was of critical importance.

"I agree. I came out here intending to learn about my child—if she is, indeed, mine—not to commune in the dark with the local earthworms."

"Better you talk to them, you've got so much in common," Annabel shot back, unreasonably hurt by his words. "Let me remind you that I'm not the one who sent for you, so never mind your nasty little slurs about whether or not you're her father."

"It's true, you didn't send for me, which is precisely why I tend to believe she is my daughter. Oh no, Annabel—" His fingers closed again, gentle and irrevocable, not around her hand this time, but around the back of her neck, forcing her to remain crouched down beside him. "—you're not escaping me now. I've made fools enough of both of us, so we might as well finish our business and have done with it."

"What *business*? What do you want of me?"

Footsteps and voices were approaching, spreading around them, circling them like an ever-tightening noose.

". . . sure they went this way . . ."

"What a novel idea—a bridal treasure hunt!"

"Shouldn't we call the police or something?" Marion, scenting scandal, was practically squeaking with glee.

"Of course not."

For a moment, Annabel thought the rhododendron bush itself had spoken, so close were Jeremy's calming words. She realized he'd followed the path they'd taken and that she could almost reach out and touch him. All she had to do was call out his name, softly, and he would put a halt to this whole ridiculous situation. Obscurely, she remained silent.

"Annabel's taking a stroll in the garden is hardly a matter for the police, Aunt Marion," Jeremy went on, and with inexplicable relief, Annabel heard his voice fade as he shepherded the guests back up to the terrace. "I think we should all go inside and . . ."

Gradually, the quiet sounds of night resumed and the tension she didn't know had crept up on her dissipated under the soothing massage of Luke's fingers. "I don't know about you, Annabel," he whispered in her ear, "but I'm getting too old to be meeting like this. Can't we find some place more comfortable for our talk?"

"Well, I suppose—"

"Someplace private. I don't want any more interruptions."

Heavens, neither did she! She hadn't spent the better part of the last ten years being a model of worthy virtue, to have him stroll on the scene at the last moment and set her whole world on its ears.

Swiveling her head, she cast him a glance, intent only on conveying her utter annoyance with him, and found herself, instead, rediscovering the face of the man who was, indubitably, Pandora's father. It was unnerving. Perhaps by some trick of the moonlight, he appeared at once a stranger and someone dearly familiar; someone she'd loved for ten years. The impact of that realization staggered her.

My stars, she thought, *but he is handsome!* No wonder she'd fallen under his spell, all those years ago.

"Stop appealing to me with those great blue-black eyes of yours," Luke advised her, his voice stabbing her little bubble of euphoria in less than a blink. "The last time we huddled together in the dark like this, you got me into all sorts of trouble."

"Me!" Indignation sent her voice soaring into a whispered shriek. "There was only one sort of trouble, Luke Barrington—the kind nice girls don't get into, not if they've got half the brains they were born with—and guess who got lucky. Do you have *any* idea what it was like for me, coming home from my holiday and finding myself pregnant by a man who'd left no forwarding address?"

"Not the slightest," he replied mildly. "How could I? I'm not a mind reader, never pretended to be."

"If you're implying that I should've found you somehow, and come to you with my 'trouble'—flung myself on your charity—"

"Cut the dramatics, Annabel. I had a right to be kept informed."

"A man in your situation was hardly entitled to any rights with another woman. You belonged to someone else at that time, as I recall. Not that you bothered to tell me that until after you'd seduced me, but you did make quite a point of it . . . later."

"But when you flung yourself at me, we didn't know

26

there would be any 'later,' so you can hardly blame me for giving the 'here and now' all my attention."

Flung herself at him? Outraged, Annabel swallowed a great deal more night air than her lungs could comfortably accommodate. "You conceited pig," she choked. "I remember full well how you came on to me. Good grief, you were all hands to say the least. I'm lucky I didn't have twins."

Luke sighed with irritating forbearance. "The propagation of twins depends on something more than hands, as you should know. Look, sweetheart, I'm sorry I ever started this. Have some pity, and save the recriminations for later. I'm forty years old now, not twenty-nine, and the intervening years haven't been kind. Too much skiing and football have left me with bad knees, and though you probably think it's no more than I deserve, kneeling in damp earth like this is hell on my arthritis. Let's find someplace else to catch up on our individual shortcomings."

To Annabel's way of thinking, the shortcomings had been all his. She'd been little more than a child at the time she'd stumbled across him, and terrified for her life. Protecting her virtue had seemed of minor significance compared with the immediate perils of survival that had been confronting her.

Maui, in the early grip of a tsunami that was to tear palm trees up by their roots and wash out roads, had been a far cry from the tropical paradise depicted on all the travel posters. Napili, with its gentle crescent of white beach and turquoise waters, had become, without warning, a howling banshee of swirling sand and outraged breakers wreaking destruction on everything they encountered.

Returning late from a camping trip on the edge of

27

the crater atop Haleakala, Annabel had finally reached her rented condominium only to find herself alone and without electricity or phone. Blinded by sand, she'd been fighting her way back to her car in the hope of reaching the nearest hurricane shelter, when the skies had opened and let fly with such a torrent of rain that the Ark itself would have been the only viable mode of transportation. With the ocean raging at her back, the threat of a tidal wave explicit in its fury, and the wall of rain in front of her, she was effectively marooned and dependent entirely on her own resources. And it was then, in the premature dusk of the storm, that she'd felt the first twinges of fear gnawing at her spine.

When the beams of an approaching vehicle had penetrated the dying yellow light, she'd been so grateful to find she was not, after all, the only person left on the island, that she would have welcomed the arrival of Jack the Ripper himself. But it had been Luke Barrington instead—and that had turned out to be the greatest hazard of all.

"If you'd let go of my neck," she suggested now, without a trace of sympathy, "you could creak to your feet and follow me to the garden shed. That should be private enough to satisfy even you."

He gave a soft snort of laughter. "Do much entertaining there, Annabel?"

"Never before," she returned witheringly, "but it's good enough for you. Come on."

"Yes, ma'am."

The Pryce garden shed, Luke shortly discovered, would have been considered palatial accommodation in some corners of the world. He'd had no idea the family was so well-heeled, although he should have

28

guessed, considering the stationery Pandora had used. *Pandora?* Good God, what had the child done to deserve such a name? No matter, the point was, whatever her reasons for bringing him into the picture at this late date, they clearly weren't fiscal. And he had to admit, he was a little upset by that. It would have been a hell of a lot easier to maintain some sort of distance and perspective had he been met by a precocious child, aided and abetted in her schemes by a money-grubbing mother. But this diaphanous creature confronting him now, with her pale and flawless skin and soft, brown hair, was about as far removed from conniving as it was possible to be and still remain mortal. She must be about thirty, yet she looked barely old enough to conceive, let alone be a parent. Which reminded him: "Where is my daughter, Annabel?"

"I don't keep her in here, Luke. Now that she's housebroken, she's allowed to live with us."

The biting restraint of her reply absolutely cracked him up. And put another dent in his armor. A shrew he would have found entirely resistible, an empty-headed socialite likewise, but this endearingly nervous woman, shaking inside her designer dress, betrayed a spirit and intelligence that captivated him. Smothering his laughter, he replied. "Well, since she's so socially acceptable, I think I'd like to meet her. How soon can that be arranged?"

The question sparked a terrible fear in Annabel. What if he tried to take Pandora away from her?

He can't, she reasoned. Pandora is old enough to decide for herself where she wants to live, and I'm her mother. She'll choose me.

But it was Pandora—sneakily, behind Annabel's back—who'd initiated contact with her father. Why?

And why now? Was she really so averse to having Jeremy as her stepfather that she'd rather live with a total stranger? Were the ties that bound mother and child so frail that they could be severed this easily, when all Annabel had wanted was to give her daughter a normal family environment? Distressed, Annabel leaned her head against the wall, her mind reeling with the possibilities and implications arising from Luke's appearance.

"Well, Annabel? Where is the child?"

"The child," she temporized, unable to cope with questions that she was afraid to answer, "has a name."

"I know. Poor little thing, I feel sorry for her. Couldn't you have come up with something more ordinary than Pandora?"

Anyone less in need of sympathy than Pandora was hard to envision. Annabel wished she had a fraction of her daughter's aplomb. "Ordinary names are for ordinary people, and there is nothing ordinary about my daughter."

"That I can believe." In the slightly musty atmosphere of the shed, Annabel's perfume whispered toward him, spicy and exotic, jarring him into fresh and poignant awareness of her. He remembered her scent full well the night she'd become pregnant with his child, the bouquet of crushed hibiscus and frangipani carried on the wind and washed through her hair by the rain. It had intoxicated him, just as this other, more sophisticated perfume threatened to do now.

Carefully, he stepped away from her, daunted by the realization that, with very little encouragement, history could well repeat itself. "Let's dispense with all this wheel-spinning," he said, turning his mind firmly to the real issue between them. "I want to see my

30

child, and I want to know why you never told me about her before now."

"When I met you," Annabel informed him, the curtness of his tone inspiring her to dish out in full measure as much as he was prepared to fling at her, "you were engaged to whatever-her-name was and you made it abundantly clear that our little affair ended the day you boarded that plane for Toronto. By the time Pandora was born, you were married to what's-her-name—"

"Melinda."

"Hah! And you've got the nerve to criticize my choice of names? Anyhow, by the time Pandora was born, you were married to Belinda—"

"*Me*linda."

"Oh, shut up! Melinda, Belinda, either way, I can imagine with what delight she'd have welcomed us showing up on your doorstep."

"Are you telling me, Annabel, that if I'd been free to do the honorable thing and marry you, you'd have tracked me down and made an honest man of me—not to mention legitimizing our child?"

"It wasn't a choice I ever had," she insisted miserably, his words reviving a shame that had taken her years to overcome."

"Oh, but it was. Melinda and I never made it to the altar. She married my best friend, six months after I got back from Hawaii. So if sacrifice was your intent, I'm afraid it was a wasted effort."

What? All that humiliation, all that breast-beating, for nothing? All that weeping in the privacy of the night, for someone she'd never believed was hers to take? She could have killed him for enlightening her now. "I didn't need you," she spat, lying through her

31

teeth. "There was no reason to chase you down, regardless of whether or not you were married."

Well, she had certainly managed without him, and done it not too badly, from what he could tell. It didn't do a great deal for his ego to discover how dispensable he'd been. "There's such a thing as taking responsibility for one's own, you know," he chided her gently.

That he was the absent Pandora's father, Luke realized, was no longer something he doubted. No man in his right mind could misconstrue Annabel's dismay at his arrival; anyone less eager to saddle him with paternal obligations he could scarcely imagine. If it had been left to her, he'd have died an old man without knowing he was a father. Talk about planned obsolescence!

"You never married? Never had other children?" he asked, intrigued, despite himself, by the woman as much as by the child she'd borne.

"A single mother isn't exactly a sought-after commodity in most men's eyes. In any case, I had my hands full with a baby to look after, and a career to establish. Marriage wasn't exactly a priority, until now."

"So you've been alone all these years?" A sense of waste, of loss, reared up in him, and left him thoroughly confused. He didn't understand why he should feel as though he'd held the winning ticket in a lottery, and not had the good sense to check his number in time to claim his prize.

"No, I've lived with my mother."

"No father? No brothers or sisters?"

"I'm an only child." Annabel moved away, toward the door of the shed. How slight an impression she must have made on him eleven years ago, that he remembered so little of what she'd told him. They'd spent four days talking and . . . Oh, damn him for coming back and souring all her present contentment with vague regrets. "My father died when I was nine. My mother is my only close relative. She helped me raise Pandora."

Then God help Pandora, he thought uncharitably. What sort of person was she growing into, insulated in this house of women? "Didn't it ever strike you that she deserved a more normal upbringing, Annabel?"

The displeasure in his voice inflamed her. She spun around, the filmy skirt of her dress flaring out and snagging on the rough cedar siding of the wall. "Of course it did," she replied with deceptive equanimity, "but that doesn't mean I was willing to settle for anyone, just to give her a father. I waited for the right man to come along, and I found Jeremy. Believe me, he was worth waiting for." She stopped to draw breath, and wished she felt as sure as she sounded, then continued: "So, if it's concern for Pandora's welfare that's brought you charging out here, you can climb on your big white horse and gallop back to wherever it is you came from."

"Under the nearest rock?" he suggested with the dry humor. "My, my, Annabel, if you'd been this prickly and standoffish in Hawaii, there wouldn't be any Pandora to worry about. Here, let me help you."

Impeded by the gloom, Annabel struggled without success to free her skirt. "If I don't get back to the party," she muttered, taking out her frustration on the delicate fabric, "people really will start to wonder."

"They'll wonder even more, if you appear in your slip. For Pete's sake, stand still and let me play unwelcome knight to a damsel in distress one last time."

33

Then, sensing her uncertainty, he added slyly; "Do you want your guests to think you've been up to some sort of hanky-panky, showing up with your clothes all torn?"

The mere thought gave her palpitations. "Heavens, no!" she gasped, and surrendered the task to him.

Kneeling beside her, he swept up a handful of the dress, the better to view the damage, and was at once diverted by the proximity of feminine hips and limbs swathed in pink chiffon, no more than an inch from his nose. Those perfumed curves . . . Even in the dim light, there was no mistaking their allure. There they were, beguilingly revealed by the friendly moon, all opalescent, silken elegance.

"They creaked," Annabel observed, with faint malicious glee, somewhere above his head. "I heard them. Your knees actually creaked." It was the most cheerful remark she'd made to him all evening.

"Ha, ha," he replied in sepulchral tones, not at all amused. He thanked God he was kneeling; at least that spared him the indignity of falling down. Bad enough to be drooling like a pervert, his eyes riveted to the fabric skimming her thighs with a familiarity that was criminal. No woman should be allowed such legs. All by themselves, they could drive a man to madness.

Desire turned his fingers to thumbs. Without deliberate intent, he found his hands blundering against her knee, and was so enchanted with its delicacy that he sought the other, fully conscious, then, that he was trespassing into very dangerous territory.

"Get on with it," Annabel whispered, impatient.

"Well," he murmured, "If you insist." And blatantly slid one palm behind her knee, his fingers discovering the smooth curve of her calf with telling delight.

34

Annabel let out a muffled shriek and rapped him smartly on the skull with her knuckles, at the same time spinning away from him. There was no mistaking the resultant damage to her dress as the chiffon tore neatly from hem to mid-thigh.

Dazed, and more than a little embarrassed, Luke sprang to his feet, prepared to endure whatever vituperation she heaped on him. He certainly deserved it. What had possessed him, groping around in the dark like a horny adolescent? He felt like an idiot. "Annabel—" he began, sincerely apologetic.

The anger he'd expected, however, simply didn't materialize. Far from repelling him, she squealed softly and, covering her face with her hands, flung herself into his arms. Gratified and astonished, he held her close. He didn't pretend to understand her, but he wasn't fool enough to pass up the chance to get close to her. After all, she was the mother of his child. "There, there," he soothed, enfolding her more securely.

But her agitation grew. "Ugh!" she wailed, cringing and swiping frantically at her head. "Spiders' webs—all in my hair. Are there any on me?"

"Webs?" he asked, bewildered.

"Spiders, you fool!"

Deflated, he released her, the moment losing all its magic. If he had any role to play in her life, it wasn't romantic—at least not at this point. Disturbed more than he cared to admit at the feelings she stirred in him, he summoned his most avuncular attitude and turned his mind to the matter at hand. "Let me see, Annabel."

It merely added to his confusion when she turned on him like a wildcat.

"Oh, never mind!" To her rage, her voice cracked and tears overflowed her eyes to roll down her face. "Look what you've done to me!" she sobbed. "My dress is ruined, my hair's a mess, and God only knows what everyone up at the house must be thinking."

Annabel dear, a little voice inside her protested. *This isn't like you. Get a grip.*

But the sobs gathered momentum and she abandoned herself to her growing misery, since there seemed no way around it. "I'm getting m-m-married the week after next, and you show up—Pandora's father—" She drew in a long, hiccupping breath. "On top of everything else, I hardly know you. What am I supposed to do now?"

He would curse himself later, he knew, but how else did a man respond to a woman, when her tears made silver tracks over her Romanian-Russian cheekbones and her mouth looked like a bruised rosebud? "Well, Annabel," he whispered over the drumming of his heart, "the last, I can do something about." When he pulled her to him this time, she leaned against him, all her resistance seemingly spent.

She never meant to let him kiss her. It just seemed to happen, as naturally as breathing—though why she should think that, when it was all she could do to draw breath, was a mystery. He sort of nudged her head with his chin so that she lifted her face to his, and he laid his lips softly on hers, to comfort her.

The trouble was, he didn't let it end when it should have. His mouth lingered, the utter harmony of its touch alerting her to a finer rapture, if only she were brave enough to admit it. Something that she didn't want to recognize stirred inside Annabel and began to flourish again. Terrified, she let her eyes fly open as

36

though, by staring him right in the face, she could deny Luke's influence over her.

"Close your eyes, Annabel," he told her with quiet authority, his mouth still grazing hers, and without demur, she obeyed. His breath feathered over her lips, and then he resumed the kiss at the same persuasive level.

Oh, God, was her last coherent thought, *please help me!*

But God was busy elsewhere, and she was left to her own resources. Mindlessly, Annabel let salvation elude her. Her arms slid around Luke's neck and urged him closer until all of her, not just her mouth, was imprinted against him. With a spontaneity she thought she'd outgrown, she let herself hang trembling on the brink of the kiss, aware only that beyond it lay a world of unimaginable and forbidden pleasures.

Ribbons of desire undulated between them, and it was all Luke could do to contain himself. For a small eternity, he held her lips with his, a glimmer of awareness for all that he'd missed and that Jeremy was about to inherit, leaving an ache where he thought his heart used to be. Then, he stepped back, removing her arms from around his neck. "Do you know me any better now?" he inquired, striving for a lightness that had become increasingly elusive in the last half hour. "Enough, perhaps, to introduce me to my daughter?"

CHAPTER THREE

"Now? Like this?" Aghast, Annabel stared at him, all the tiny electricities he'd generated petering out as practicality took control again.

He coughed, and discreetly looked away from the fetching exposure of lace revealed by the tear in her skirt. "I see what you mean. Your dress . . . I don't think it will ever be the same again."

Nothing would ever be the same again, she lamented silently. Couldn't he see that the dress was the least of her concerns? "How do I introduce you?"

"She already knows who I am."

"I don't mean Pandora." What an obtuse individual he was. "A room full of people saw me disappear into the night with you. How do I account for that? And what possible reasons do I have for changing my clothes halfway through a party?"

He turned toward her again, his eyes gleaming darkly. "Well," he drawled, pure seductive evil in his tone, "you could tell everyone—"

"Never mind," she snapped. "I can come up with my own excuses. If you will please get out of my way, I'll go up to my room by the back stairs, and you . . ." She lifted her hands despairingly. How did one explain the presence of an anonymous ex-lover when one was shortly to become another man's bride?

"I shall go back to the party," Luke decided for her, "and mingle sociably with the crowd. And if anyone asks me who I am, I'll simply tell them—"

"Don't you dare!"

"That I'm an out-of-town relative, here to join the festivities, and to wish you and your groom well."

An entirely plausible explanation. Truthful, even. Why, then, did she feel she was up to her knees in quicksand, and sinking fast? "Excuse me," she muttered, and sidled by him as if she feared he might contaminate her. "Wait here a couple of minutes. I don't want you following too close behind me."

She ducked out of the door and prepared to slip away in the dark. "Watch out for webs," he called after her.

"Drop dead," she advised him tartly, and scuttled off between the rows of manicured shrubs, ragged ends of pink chiffon trailing around her ankles.

As it happened, the french doors by which he'd left were closed when he reached the terrace, and it struck Luke that he'd make a more unobtrusive entrance if he came in through the main body of the house. The front door, flanked by brass carriage lanterns, stood wide and welcoming. Stopping briefly before a mirror in the hall, he checked his reflection for lipstick stains, and tugged his jacket more snugly over his shoulders. Behind him, a curved staircase rose to the bedrooms, and in one of them, Annabel was even now taking off her clothes. He found the prospect delicious.

Next to the stairs, a door suddenly opened. Guiltily, he checked the mirror one last time and decided he'd pass inspection. No telltale signs that he'd been doing anything untoward with the bride. He could look the groom in the eye and not turn a hair.

Swinging around, he found himself confronted by a woman it was impossible not to recognize. "You're Annabel's mother," he said.

Sybil, resplendent in scarlet silk, came to stand directly in front of him, the better to examine him with those unmistakable navy-blue eyes. "And you," she replied, "are Pandora's father."

He felt as if he'd known her for years; as if they were very old and very good friends. "It's that obvious?"

"Clear as the nose on your face," she declared, her eyes dancing. "Almost. Pandora's isn't quite as . . . mature."

He laughed outright at that. "I'm afraid I chose a bad time to arrive, Mrs. Pryce."

She touched a hand to her hair. "Not at all," she assured him graciously. "We were expecting you."

"We?"

By way of reply, she inclined her head and raised her brows. Out of the corner of his eye, he saw the mirrored image of a small person descending the stairs. To his absolute amazement, he was consumed with sudden and acute anxiety. Swallowing, he turned and looked at his daughter for the first time.

Oh my God! he thought, swamped by myriad emotions.

She was thin and solemn; angular and plain; feminine and beautiful. She had Annabel's pale, ash-brown hair, and his mother's eyes. They were full of suspicion and intelligence and reserve. She was a total stranger, but in a crowd of thousands, it seemed to him he'd have known her immediately. The revelation

40

left him weak, all his assurance and *savoir faire* evaporated. "Well," he said, and heard his voice emerge rusty as an old man's, "hello. I'm Luke Barrington."

"Give me strength," Pandora sighed, rolling her eyes at Sybil. "Wouldn't you think, Grandmother, after all these years, he could've said 'Father'?"

Sybil cast him a sympathetic glance. "Be patient, my lamb," she counseled Pandora. "A daughter is a new concept for him. You, on the other hand, have been used to the idea of a father all your life."

Pandora sighed again, and looked at him patronizingly. "I suppose," she conceded, and advanced to within touching distance. "You may kiss me."

Luke felt like declining. She may have her mother's hair, and his mother's eyes, but her mouth was all her own. He wondered why he'd ever felt the slightest twinge of pity for this self-possessed little creature. While he was wiping damp palms on the seat of his pants, she was appraising him as coolly as if he were a piece of horseflesh about to be auctioned off. The notion of racing out here to acquaint himself with this child struck him, suddenly, as not such a hot idea.

"Well?"

Look at her, hanging her little face out for him, a princess awaiting homage from a peon! "If you'd like me to," he returned, and was furious to hear himself almost stuttering. Bending down, he placed his lips on her cool, translucent cheek.

She suffered the embrace in silence, and he straightened quickly, feeling like a damn fool. Whatever her reasons for informing him of her existence, they clearly had no more to do with an overpowering need to know her father than they had with money. He felt

41

about as welcome as warts on a debutante. Helplessly, he turned to Sybil. "Mrs. Pryce . . . ?"

"Yes," she said. "At once. The bar's this way. My name, by the way, is Sybil."

"What about me?" Pandora wanted to know.

"You're too young to drink," Sybil decided, after momentary consideration.

Pandora was not amused. "But he's here because I sent for him."

Summoned to the royal presence, Luke thought, half entertained despite his uneasiness. I wonder what her plans are, now that she's got me here?

"Later, Pandora." Taking his arm, Sybil prepared to lead him into the living room. "Your father only just arrived, and he's three hours ahead of us. Let's give him time to recover from his jet lag, at least, before we start rearranging his life."

Pandora planted herself squarely in front of her grandmother, so that Sybil had no choice but to stop. Given the same circumstances, Luke thought he might well have opted for stepping on the child. "We don't have much time, Grandmother," she insisted ominously.

A fine sweat broke out on his forehead. Christ, what had the pair of them in store for him? "Look," he said, in as offhand a tone as he could muster, "all I know is that I received a letter telling me I had a daughter I knew nothing about, and that it was imperative I come out here because you needed me. If it's all the same to you, I'd just as soon be brought into the picture now as later."

"No, you wouldn't," Sybil declared emphatically. "You'd rather have a drink and a good night's rest, first. Pandora—"

42

"But Grandmother—!"

"Pandora, go find your mother and tell her we have another guest."

"Why—"

"Now, dear heart—before I forget I'm opposed to violence as a form of discipline."

To Luke's relief, the child obeyed, disappearing whence she came. She should be in bed anyway. It was close to ten o'clock. Children her age didn't belong at adult gatherings. "She's very . . . composed, isn't she?"

Sybil's answering smile was so brief, he wondered if he'd imagined it. "She's very much like her mother, at times. Everything hidden inside, and nothing showing on the outside. It's the Russian influence; my husband's family were inclined to brood. Then again, she's also very like us Irish—headstrong, to say the least. Oh, look, here's Annabel now. I wonder why she changed into that old thing?"

Glancing up, Luke saw Annabel poised halfway down the stairs, one hand balanced on the curving bannister, her chin lifted defiantly. She wore a black dress, stunningly simple and complemented by black hose and shoes.

"Should I introduce you?" Sybil asked, archly.

Luke fought to suppress a grin, suddenly feeling much more cheerful. "We've already met," he replied out of the side of his mouth, and feasted his eyes on Annabel's hips as they swayed toward him.

"Then I'll leave you to get reacquainted."

"What did you say to my mother?" Annabel demanded, gimlet-eyed at Sybil's hasty retreat.

Luke's grin blossomed. "You in mourning again, Miz Scarlett?" he drawled. "Seems to me, if you are, you might at least wait till you've married the poor guy, before you bury him."

"That's a disgusting thing to say."

"I dare say, but you make such a gorgeous widow, I can't seem to help myself."

"Shut your mouth," she told him. "I'm an engaged person."

"Well, hot damn, Annabel, you could've fooled me! The way you came slinking down those stairs struck me as nothing short of inviting. I do declare, I'm all in an uproar."

"Stop fancying yourself, Luke Barrington. You just don't have the ears to play Rhett Butler." Quelling words, but sadly undermined by the giggle she couldn't quite contain. His southern drawl was appalling, but the smile in those pewter-gray eyes completely disarmed her. Had she really come slinking down the stairs? And if she had, why wasn't she feeling embarrassed, instead of so pleasingly sinful? Ms. Annabel Pryce wasn't the slinky, giggly type. Sedate and sober was a more fitting description. Remembering that, she pinched her lips into a straight line, and considered the discomfort brought about by the action no less than she deserved.

Luke leaned toward her confidentially. "I met our daughter, and I don't think I made much of an impression. What have you told her about me?"

The inclination to be amused by him vanished as suddenly as it had arisen. She opened her mouth to reply, then spying Jeremy advancing her way, closed it again, paling visibly.

"Cat got your tongue, Annabel?" Luke asked.

". . . um . . . um . . ." Jeremy was bearing down on her with no intention, this time, of getting waylaid.

44

Marion, determined to miss nothing, was hot on his heels. To Annabel's consternation, there was no way of escaping either of them, unless she was to retreat up the stairs again. "Oh, good grief! Here comes my fiancé and his aunt. I shall have to introduce you."

"Yes," Luke agreed calmly. "I'm afraid you will. And you'll have to tell them why you're all in black, too. I can hardly wait to hear what you have to say."

"If you must know, I don't feel particularly proud of the way I behaved in the shed," she muttered irately, "and it's spoiled the party mood for me."

"Ah! This is the closest you can come to sackcloth and ashes. Are you planning to explain that to the fiancé?"

"Are you out of your mind? I wouldn't dare."

Luke smiled. "I would," he said.

Annabel felt her heart miss a beat, and looked at him searchingly. He surely wouldn't deliberately try to sabotage her relationship with Jeremy? "Don't joke about things like that," she begged in the seconds before the others came within hearing range.

Approaching, Jeremy took her hand. "I missed you, Annabel," he observed, examining her closely. "Where did you disappear to?"

"I . . . ah . . . um . . . my dress . . ." God in heaven, the way the three of them had their gazes glued to her face was robbing her of her wits!

"My dear," Marion was eager to inform her, "you can't imagine what went through our minds, when you disappeared that way. What happened?"

"Tell her," Luke suggested, barely moving his lips.

To Annabel's right, Jeremy's hazel eyes were flecked green with concern. Ashamed, she looked away. A fine

45

woman she was, hiding out in the garden shed with another man, practically on her wedding eve, and permitting him all sorts of liberties—not to mention the illicit pleasure she'd experienced. But Luke hadn't even the grace to look embarrassed. Instead, he stood there, bold as brass, eyeing her mouth so intently that he had it spilling forth all sorts of inanities.

"What about your dress?" Jeremy prompted.

"It's a distant relative," she replied, her thoughts scrambling to catch up with her runaway tongue.

To her left, Luke sniggered. "Annabel, do you think you could compose yourself enough to introduce me to your fiancé?"

"Luke Barrington," she hastily amended, "is a distant relative, and I spilled a drink on my dress."

Jeremy seemed to take notice of Luke for the first time. The two men were much of a height, something over six feet, and at five four, Annabel felt at a decided disadvantage. "Barrington?" Jeremy repeated. "I don't believe I've heard you mentioned before."

"I don't believe you have," Luke informed him, the merest suggestion of belligerence in the set of his jaw, in the subtle tension of his shoulders, neither of which was quite countered by the geniality of his smile. "Annabel and I haven't been close in some years, but there's nothing like a wedding for bringing people together again."

They were on dangerously thin ice, Annabel thought in panic. Next, he'd be regaling everyone with an account of how they first met, and although Pandora clearly had to have been fathered by someone, Annabel had never felt inclined to elaborate on the details. They were part of a past she'd convinced her-

46

self was no longer relevant to the present. The fact that, since Luke's reappearance, the past and the present were becoming part of a whole that seemed bent on redesigning the future, was something she found most disturbing. Jeremy, with his keen surgeon's eye, was likely to pick up on such feelings, and now was scarcely an appropriate time to bare her soul, especially not with Marion hyperventilating in the background.

"I see." Jeremy rested thoughtful eyes on Luke for a moment, then turned back to Annabel. "Why don't we all join the others, darling?"

"Yes, darling, why don't we?" Luke murmured in her left ear.

Annoyance stopped her in her tracks, and restored clarity to her thoughts. "Please go ahead without us," she said to Jeremy, including Marion in her politely uttered request. "Luke and I were almost finished catching up on the news when you found us. We'll join you in a few minutes."

Again that thoughtful look from Jeremy. Oh my, but he saw entirely too much. "Please?" she said again.

He acquiesced with a nod, and taking his aunt by the elbow, steered her in the direction of the living room. The moment they were out of earshot, Annabel spun on Luke. "You listen to me," she raged in quiet fury, "because I mean every word I'm about to say. I don't know why you're here, but whatever the reason, you will not upset my life a second time, nor will you hurt the people I love. I'm not the meek little innocent you seduced eleven years ago. I've worked hard to get to where I am today, and you're not going to step in now and spoil things for me."

47

"Where *are* you, Annabel?" Luke asked, his eyes behind their glasses penetratingly observant. It made her squirm.

"I'm at peace," she told him, "and I have my future all mapped out. There aren't any unwelcome surprises in it, which sort of makes you redundant, don't you think? I know exactly where I'm going, and I don't intend to let anything deflect me."

"Is that what you think I'm trying to do?"

"Why else are you here?"

The question left him looking thoroughly taken aback. "Damned if I thought I knew," he admitted, running a hand through his hair, "until an hour ago."

"The point is—"

"The point is, my darling Annabel, that you're not as easy to overlook as I'd expected. I thought Pandora was the main reason I was here. But now I'm so bloody confused by the way you make me feel that I'm hardly responsible for anything I say or do."

He reached out and touched her hand almost diffidently. "I find myself wondering why I ever let you go," he murmured, and at his words and his look, all the fire went out of her. "What do you suppose would have happened if we'd kept in touch, after Hawaii?"

Annabel closed her eyes, hoping by doing so, she could shut out the treacherous alternatives that came to mind. "Please don't say these things, not now. It's too late for regrets."

"It's never too late," he contradicted her gently. "Only fools and dead men believe that."

"Then I'm a fool and intend remaining one. And now, let's join the others. Since you're here, I suppose I'll have to introduce you—as a distant relative." She tossed him a resentful glance. "By the time anyone thinks to question the relationship, you will, hopefully, have left."

"Don't count on it, Annabel."

To her chagrin, he was an instant hit with everyone, and her fear that he wouldn't just fade into the woodwork crystallized into certainty. Sybil, taking her cue from Annabel's introductions, flung herself so convincingly into the role of one newly reunited with long-lost kinfolk that it was beyond any outsider's ability to believe otherwise.

She'll be hauling in the fatted calf next, Annabel thought sourly, and went to stand beside Jeremy. When she caught Luke's gaze on her, she slipped her hand through Jeremy's arm and smiled up at him as if she thought the sun rose and set on his face. Dismayingly, when he responded by dropping a kiss on the tip of her nose, she found her eyes slewing around to watch the effect on Luke. And he, contrary creature, was busily charming some blond woman and totally oblivious to the scene being enacted especially for his benefit.

The little streak of jealousy this produced in Annabel left her badly shaken. She didn't consider herself the sort of person who normally sank to such petty levels. She'd never known a moment's envy or unrest with Jeremy, for heaven's sake, and she was engaged to him. Luke Barrington was at liberty to ogle whomever he pleased, as long as he kept his distance from her.

Still, she couldn't suppress her satisfaction when Blondie was displaced by Jeremy's aunt. Marion wouldn't be such a pushover. It would take more than a well-flossed smile to slide past her. The woman oozed suspicion, and had a nose for ferreting out smooth operators that would put a bloodhound to shame. Appeased, Annabel turned her back. This time, Luke had met his match.

"Stockbroker!" Marion trilled from across the room, and it was more than human nature could endure not to look around. There was Marion, her smile almost as expansive as her bosom, hanging on Luke's words as if she thought the wisdom of the ages was about to be poured in her ear. "My dear young man, how very impressive. Are you terribly successful?"

"Terribly," Luke replied, turning on her the full barrage of a smile that, even from across the room, unleashed in Annabel all sorts of vague yearnings that she would have much preferred remain dormant. Her face ached from smiling at people she scarcely knew, and the evening, which should have been so delightful, had become an ordeal which couldn't end soon enough.

"Annabel," Jeremy said, nodding toward the door, "I think your mother's trying to catch your eye. People are starting to leave, and I suppose we should go say our good-byes."

"Thank God," Annabel breathed, with more relief than was socially correct. "I thought they were going to stay all night." As some were, Aunt Marion included. Jeremy's penthouse had only one guest bedroom, which his parents were occupying, but the Pryce house could accommodate a fair number of guests. One more, in fact, than Annabel had bargained for, as she discovered when she finally joined her mother.

"I invited Luke to stay here," Sybil whispered. "It seemed the most sensible idea."

Sensible? Sometimes, Annabel wondered if her mother had full command of her faculties. Having Luke under the same roof struck her as potentially disastrous. "There are plenty of hotels in town," she protested.

But Sybil wouldn't budge. "We have room here, my darling, and it would be ungracious to send the poor man off to a hotel after he's traveled so far to find you. He seemed most appreciative of the offer."

Of course he did, the conniving weasel! What better vantage point from which to observe the ripple effect of his presence? Annabel felt, in that moment, that she was looking at the tip of an iceberg, and that the full extent of the danger this man posed to her peace of mind was only partially revealed.

". . . so nice to have met you, Mrs. Carson . . . tomorrow, perhaps, for lunch? . . ." She didn't know how she managed to dredge up the appropriate responses as Jeremy's parents took their leave. His mother, a pretty woman, was content to kiss the air in the vicinity of Annabel's cheek, and pat her hand, but the senior Dr. Carson was another matter entirely. Possessed of the same observant eye as his son, he took full stock of Annabel's features and seemed able to see clear through her, to the teeming mass of anxiety and doubt and confusion that were casting such a pall on her pre-wedding celebrations. He exited shaking his head.

Uttering the barest civility of a farewell, Annabel closed the door on the lot of them with what she feared was unseemly haste. She knew, if she'd dallied a minute longer in polite chit-chat, she'd have started babbling again, and she'd done enough of that tonight to last her a lifetime.

51

"You're a troublemaker, Mother," she accused Sybil, noting that they were alone in the hall and that everyone else had apparently retired to bed.

"One does one's best, dear heart," Sybil murmured, her face wreathed in the most beatific of smiles.

"I beg your pardon?"

"You need your rest." Sybil tried to appear solicitous and succeeded only in looking smug. "Do go to bed, Annabel. You look like death warmed over."

Who wouldn't, Annabel wondered as she climbed the stairs, if her own mother and daughter were in league with the devil? Especially when he took the form of Luke Barrington?

Dispirited, she let herself into her room and kicked off her shoes. The bedraggled pink chiffon dress hung over the back of a chair, reminding her of her narrow escape in the garden shed. The memory of Luke's kiss made her weak-kneed all over again. Just as well he hadn't persisted; heaven only knew how far things might have gone.

Releasing the zipper, she let the black dress fall around her ankles and stepped out of it, her fingers kneading the tension in her neck. The day had surely lasted forty-eight hours, and tomorrow promised to be no better.

She was seated at her dressing table, her hair scraped back, her face covered with globs of cleansing cream, when she happened to glance in the mirror at the room behind her, and saw a pair of masculine legs, crossed at the ankle, the feet dangling off the end of the bed. It never occurred to her to scream or betray the least sign of alarm. Instead, she raised her eyes to his face, resignation a leaden weight inside her.

"Take your time, Annabel my love," Luke said

softly, crossing his hands behind his head and settling himself more comfortably against the pillows. "Don't neglect your wrinkles on my account. I can wait a few minutes longer for your undivided attention."

CHAPTER FOUR

It was pointless to give vent to her outrage at his flagrant invasion of her privacy. To indulge herself by expressing it would serve no purpose beyond altering the rest of the household to Luke's presence in her bedroom. That sort of limelight she didn't need. He was implacably there, and she knew quite well that she could never embarrass him into leaving. As for appealing to his better nature—she wasn't sure he had one. In any case, if there had to be a confrontation, it was as well, she supposed, that it take place here, where no one was likely to overhear.

But she wished she'd noticed him before she'd so blithely divested herself of half her clothing. Dignity was rather elusive when she was so horribly conscious of her near-naked state, especially when she was blessed with such an absorbed audience. She could feel his eyes boring right through her back, and zeroing in on her front with its thirty-year-old breasts that weren't nearly as perky as those he'd made love to in Hawaii.

Sighing, she fought the urge to cross her arms protectively, and drew on the self-control that she knew was cowering somewhere in the corner of her brain. "Go ahead and state what's on your mind," she invited, plucking a tissue from the box at her elbow, and removing the cleansing cream with careful strokes. "I can do two things at once."

"Then you're to be congratulated. Unfortunately, I don't share your talent, sweet thing, and if you keep shifting all that lovely flesh around like that, I'm very likely to forget what I really came here for, and give way to the urge to take a bite out of you."

Deliberately, Annabel picked up her hairbrush and, drawing it through the exuberant tangle of her curls, impaled his reflection in her most repressive stare. "Do try to contain yourself," she suggested loftily, "because I'd find such behavior extremely offensive. I'm not the type to be swept away by Neanderthal tactics."

"Then I take my hat off to you."

She should have heeded the glimmer that illuminated his eyes. Instead, she walked right into the trap he so neatly laid for her. "Don't bother," she scoffed, attacking the ringlets that clung at the nape of her neck with swift, upward strokes.

"No bother," he assured her, the glimmer suddenly so wickedly bright, it spread to his mouth in a slow and devastating grin. "It's a small enough gesture, considering the speed with which you stripped off for me."

Annabel wished, vehemently, that she were one of those women who could curse unblushingly without feeling like a trollop. Defiant as a child, she let loose in her mind all the wicked, unprintable words she knew —four-letter, five-, whatever it took—and hoped their message was reflected in the irate pupils of her eyes. Apparently, it was.

Luke slid off the bed in a movement so swift and lithe, he was at her shoulder before she could exhale her rage. "Darling Annabel," he purred with unconcealed delight, "we have so much in common. No wonder our little girl is such a feisty individual." And then without leave or invitation, he bent down and placed his warm and lovely mouth at the very spot where her neck flowed into the curve of her shoulder.

It was another fleeting touch. Like the kiss in the garden shed, it did no more than promise; was, in fact, more full of reverence than passion, more bent on homage than desire. Yet its effect reverberated clean to her soul and sent the hairbrush clattering over the polished walnut of her dressing table.

Composure fled and was replaced by a succession of tiny ecstasies that erupted from everywhere: the soles of her feet, and the backs of her knees where echoes of an earlier pleasure still lingered. And other, concealed places. Places she wished she didn't have to acknowledge, that she'd tried very hard to forget.

Behind her, Luke lifted his head and let his eyes slide down the fragile core of her spine until it dipped out of sight beneath the top of a camisole lavishly adorned with French lace. "Don't lean over that way, darling Annabel," he begged her, his voice drowning her with tenderness. "Unlike you, I recognize very well how susceptible I am to the weaknesses of the flesh."

His hands, until then mercifully restrained, whispered down her arms to cradle her elbows. How soft and scented she was, he thought, and didn't try to prevent himself from drawing her up and back, until she was resting against him. Her head, cushioned by the lively curls that had rioted to shoulder length when first he'd met her, settled despairingly in the hollow beneath his ribs.

Deeply moved by her absolute vulnerability, he was half ashamed of the peripheral gladness that seized him to know that discipline had kept his body firm and hard. At that fragile, breathless moment, his pride would have been scorched had he allowed himself to grow flabby and complacent as other men of forty often did. He had never suspected himself possessed of such untimely vanity.

Restively, she stirred against him, and the warm, alive feel of her brought other emotions into play, luring his fingers to test the limits of her forbearance. It was worth the risk when all he had to lose was her poor opinion of him. With infinite pleasure, he let his hands rediscover her, and found that this was not, after all, the Annabel of his youth. That long-ago girl had been springtime, lovely and full of promise for the summer yet to come. He'd never forgotten her, had succeeded only in hoarding the secret of her so that no one else would know he still possessed it. But now, in the hushed glow of this room, the new Annabel took hold of his heart and relegated the girl to the past where she belonged. He no longer needed her, because here was the woman, rich with the fulfillment of that early promise.

"Annabel, Annabel," he whispered, hoarse with confused emotion, "what did I deprive us of, the day I walked away from you?"

She raised her eyes and looked at the face mirrored above hers, and could no more deny the regret in his voice than she could ignore its sincerity. Both were stenciled in the grooves that ran beside his mouth like little rivers of pain. They could find no place to hide in the barren waste of his beautiful gray eyes. And they, as much as his magical hands, brought her to the brink of ruin, hacking all her pretty little plans to pieces.

Propriety lost out to propinquity in a battle so swift and savage there was never any doubt as to its outcome. Consigning herself to perdition, she allowed him to trespass on territory she'd promised to another man.

Shamelessly, her breasts sang with pleasure at his touch, more alive than they had any right to be. And it was she, not he, who let loose a groan of pure frustration that he elected not to slip aside the camisole strap and let the fabric fall away to reveal those same breasts —vital and eager, and so hungry for more that they throbbed with pain. She was enthralled and terrified. "I hate you," she whispered feebly, and knew that he heard the utter panic in her words.

"I know, darling," he murmured, lifting her free of the bench and ringing her around the waist with arms that threatened never to let her go. "I know just what you mean."

She spun gently inside the circle he made around her, and pushed helplessly against his chest, weak as any kitten and furious to be so. "If you kiss me," she rashly promised, "I'll never speak to you again."

To her mingled horror and delight, the bleakness that tore at her melted from his eyes and was replaced by dawning amusement. "Annabel darling, I'm surprised you have such a tiny nose, you tell such dreadful lies."

Seizing what seemed to be a reprieve, she collected herself, quivering with indignation and pursing her lips. "I most certainly do not."

He brought his arms more snugly around her and let one wicked palm slide down to define the curve of her bottom. She'd forgotten that it, too, was susceptible to seduction, and was appalled at the way it surged with anticipatory bliss. "Let's check it out," Luke suggested, and before she had time to respond, his lips sealed themselves on hers in such delicious greed that she feared she might faint.

He was the ultimate rogue, she quickly realized, for a kiss with him slid alarmingly soon into an intimate melding of angles and curves, turning all the well-disguised chinks in her armor into sweet and welcoming invitations before she could properly catch her breath. "Oh!" she sighed, tearing her mouth free of the spells he was casting, "have you no shame, coming in here and doing these things to me?"

"What is it I'm doing to you, to make you sigh, and lie, this way, Annabel?"

"I do not lie," she answered, beside herself with agitation.

"Good God," he muttered, and promptly fastened his lips over hers to silence her. And seduced her all over again.

She was desperate to regain control of a situation so far out of hand that the very floor beneath her feet seemed to be slipping away. The instant he allowed her a second to snatch a breath, she opened her mouth, intending to give him a tongue lashing he would never forget. But he was light-years ahead of her, and put his own tongue to such wicked and irresistible use that he left Annabel giddy. Perhaps the floor had slipped away; perhaps he'd taken her on a magic carpet to some other, more celestial plane. Certainly, nothing she was experiencing now bore any resemblance to the mannerly predictability of her feelings for Jeremy.

Jeremy! His face, dear and familiar and handsome, superimposed itself on the technicolor of her emotions in solid black and white, full of sadness and reproach. His eyes, possessed of an integrity she feared she lacked, would neither blink nor look away, seeing her in another man's arms. He hadn't become the fine surgeon he was by ignoring things other men might find unpleasant or painful. If betrayal was in the cards, he was the sort to take it without flinching. Unaware that she did so, Annabel uttered a whimper of shamed distress.

"What?" Luke whispered, lifting his head and leaning back to examine her. "What is it, darling Annabel?"

"Jeremy's watching," she replied.

Too much champagne, dear, the little voice inside her proclaimed. *It's making you fanciful, not to mention ridiculous. Button your lip.*

Luke was looking around as if he expected Jeremy to slide out from under the bed. "He is?"

"No."

"You're not making sense again, Annabella."

Annabel chose to ignore his corruption of her name —for the time being. "Not to you, perhaps," she conceded, disengaging his arms and putting a safe six feet of carpet between him and her. She immediately felt much better. "Meeting Pandora may be the biggest thing in your life right now, but marrying Jeremy is by far the most important event in mine. I won't allow you to spoil it."

Luke stared at her, fascinated. "I don't want to spoil things, sweet face."

"Don't call me names. Jeremy is a fine man, a won-

60

derful man. He's the kind of man any woman would give her right arm for."

"And from where I stand, that's about all he's going to get if he marries you. No, Annabel!" Seeing her about to voice more objections, Luke raised a silencing hand. "You've had your say, so now, please just shut up and let me have mine. I think it's about time we discussed the letter our daughter sent to me."

Quietly enough spoken, but the words seemed full of menace. Premonition that she wasn't going to like what she was about to hear had her scurrying nervously across the room in search of a robe. It wasn't a fitting time to be romping around unclothed. Annoyed beyond measure at how easily he'd upset her composure with his gently uttered threat, she thrust her arms into the wide sleeves of a kimono, wrapped the right front firmly over the left, and pulled the sash taut around her waist.

"Tying yourself up like a sack of potatoes on the outside won't hold you together if you're falling apart on the inside, you know," Luke offered, reclaiming his spot on her bed and leaning back with arms crossed behind his head.

Annabel flung him a baleful glare. What right had he to be so perceptive? "Oh, what do you know?" she demanded. "Nothing but what your overblown ego wants to believe. And get off my bed. You don't belong there."

"Does Jeremy?"

Another of those poisonous little questions that he slipped in, smooth as a knife. "Yes."

"Then why does Pandora feel you're marrying him solely to give her a father?"

61

"Pandora," Annabel declared with feeling, "inherited her conceit from you."

"She loves you, Annabel. I think, from the letter she sent me, that she loves you very much, and she is terribly afraid that you're settling for second best in this marriage."

His tone, unexpectedly grave and kind, and the words themselves, choked her. It was all she could do to answer him. "Don't you think I love her, too? She's my whole life and there's nothing I wouldn't do for her."

"Including marrying Jeremy, so that she can have a father?"

"No! If I'd thought having a father was all that important, I'd have contacted you, years ago."

"Well, hell's bells, Annabel, don't feel you have to beat about the bush. Just come right out and tell me I wasn't needed, and never mind bruising my ego."

His irony restored her somewhat, and the urge to howl her eyes out abated. "You simply don't understand. It's not so much that she needs a father . . . she's growing up, and I see the changes every day."

But how difficult they were to witness was something she had never bargained for. She'd thought, when she'd held her baby and marveled at the perfection that had resulted from her indiscretion, that she'd finished with pain. She'd thought that Pandora would fill the spaces left by Luke's defection. She'd thought, fool that she was, that loving a child was less heartbreaking than loving a man. But in recent months, she'd found that loving of any kind exacted a fearful price, especially when you thought it was yours for free. "She's not a little girl anymore."

Was she ever? Luke wondered, remembering the

62

self-possessed person who'd inspected him with such dispassion earlier. "That's a normal enough thing to have happen, surely?"

To his astonishment, Annabel turned huge, tragic eyes on him. "She needs me less and less. She was always independent, but in the last year, she's become more aware of the world outside this house. It's made me realize that one day, she won't be content to stay here; she'll want—"

"To fly the coop—something you've never done. Annabel, you should be glad. What do you want, a recluse? Someone who can't function without her mother holding her hand?"

"Of course not." Good Lord, what sort of parent did he think she was? "The last thing I want is to be one of those mothers who exist solely for their children. People like that end up feeling abandoned and useless. Pandora would never stand for it, and neither will I."

Luke regarded her narrowly. "I think I begin to see a game plan. Jeremy is your contingency for warding off a lonely old age."

She refused to let him needle her. "Jeremy and I share mutual needs—mutual interests. Just because we're not swooning over each other doesn't mean we don't care. Ours is a more mature kind of love."

"If that's maturity," Luke retorted, pushing his glasses on top of his head and rubbing his eyes, "then I hope I never live to experience it. Doesn't it strike you that he's too nice a guy to get shortchanged this way?"

"We're both practical people. We know what we want."

"Oh, bullshit, Annabel!" Unimpressed by her gasp

of outrage, Luke flung himself off the bed and came to stand over her. Only by a supreme effort did she restrain herself from backing away. "If you really wanted him, you could never have kissed me the way you did tonight."

"I didn't kiss you—you kissed me!" Even to her own ears, the words were childish and empty.

He looked at her scornfully. "You really are a liar— the worst kind, because you're lying to yourself. You'd like everyone to think of you as some sort of latter-day Florence Nightingale, encased in starch from head to foot, and so full of common sense it makes me want to throw up, yet underneath, you're a closet romantic who's too much of a coward to face the truth."

"You don't know the first thing about me."

"I know more than you ever will, because I'm not afraid to see what's staring me in the face." He reached inside the neck of her kimono and hooked a finger around the lace strap holding up her camisole. "White linen by day, and black lace by night, hmm?"

"What of it?"

Her skin quivered at his touch, sensation running under the surface like warm honey, but he seemed not to notice and moved past her to fling open her closet doors. "And what have we here? My goodness, so many sensible outfits! You must keep the local tailor busy year round running up these serviceable skirts and jackets. Imagine!" He swung the hangers back and forth with no regard for their contents, and swooped on the section of closet partly hidden by the mirrored doors. "But what's all this? Negligees? Silk and satin and lace? *Marabou?* Pretty kinky, Annabel, if you ask me."

"I'm not asking you. Your opinion is of no importance to me." She tried to slide the doors shut, but he fended her off with one hand, by no means done with tormenting her yet. The fragile gowns and robes swirled and fluttered in their own draft, laughing at her. "Leave my things alone—"

"And these!" He whirled around, a pair of sandals dangling from his other hand, their sequined heels flashing fire in the lamplight. "Hey, Florence, you're in the wrong business. You can't empty bedpans wearing these. They belong in the wardrobe of a dreamer —someone who still believes in fairy tales."

"Give them to me!" She drew herself up to her full sixty-four inches, trying to look regal and indifferent, and feeling, instead, horribly exposed. He towered over her, uncaring that he was shredding her to pieces with his observations. Distraught, she gave brief consideration to kicking him, very hard, in a place ladies weren't supposed to know about.

Something must have shown in her expression. He wagged a reproving finger at her. "Shame on you, Annie! Whatever happened to the sweet young thing I used to know?"

"She grew up, which is more than can be said of you."

"Oh no," he contradicted her, "she grew old before her time. Tell me, darling, why are you and Jeremy so hell-bent on racing into this middle-aged marriage of yours?"

She swept by him and picked up her ruined dress. "Jeremy and I," she declared loftily, "are not middle-aged, and neither is our marriage. We are sophisticated—something you wouldn't understand, since you're still a little boy in long pants."

"I could take them off and prove you're wrong," he

suggested helpfully, and when she scrunched the chiffon in both hands, impotent with fury, went on: "No need to take it out on the dress, love. Speaking of which, however did you come to select something so feminine? Weren't you afraid being seen in it might spoil your image?"

"I can't imagine why I bought it," she snapped, dropping it on the floor in a heap. "It was a very impractical choice. Look at how poorly it stood up to wear."

He shook with immoderate laughter, again. "Well, what do you expect, if you insist on entertaining in the garden shed? I hope you've been more sensible with your wedding outfit. None of that traditional useless stuff like gowns that trail behind you when you walk down the aisle, or grandma's old lace curtain pinned to your hair."

Annabel thought of the ecru shantung of her wedding dress, of its pure, prim lines unadorned by so much as a single ruffle. Suddenly, she hated it—even more than she hated Luke Barrington. "It's sophisticated," she informed him.

"God help us all!" He threw up his hands in despair. "In other words, you're going to look like the mother of the bride, and Jeremy, if he's lucky, might marry Sybil by mistake."

It was the last straw. "Get out of here!" she shrieked, seizing one of her black pumps and hurling it in the direction of his smug and sniggering face. "Get out of my room and out of my life."

He didn't need to duck, her aim was so bad. Instead, he backed to the door and laid one finger to his lips in a silencing gesture. "I will," he whispered, his eyes spilling with mirth. "At least until tomorrow. Now hush up, darling, before you rouse the whole house."

He opened the door quietly. From the darkened landing behind him, Aunt Marion, puffed up like an angry thrush, almost fell into the room. "Young man," she chirped, "what are you doing in our little bride's bedroom, and why is she squealing?"

If Annabel had harbored any illusions that Luke had met his match in Marion, they evaporated in that instant. "Dear lady," he crooned, lifting his shoulders in such innocent perplexity that it would have made a saint weep, "you take the words right out of my mouth. Why *are* you squealing, Annabel? Is something wrong?"

He swung back to her, pushing his glasses firmly up his nose and peering at her like a benign owl. She gaped at him, wordless with admiration. He was the most slippery weasel she'd ever encountered—and no more nearsighted, she was willing to bet, than she was. Those damned glasses were just for effect.

"Did something disturb you, my dear?" Marion, a vision in feather-bedecked slippers and matching robe, closed the door and waddled over to Annabel. "It wouldn't surprise me in the slightest. Jeremy can say what he likes; someone *was* prowling around outside the house tonight, and for all we know, he could still be out there and up to no good."

At her back, Luke rolled his eyes, shook his head in time to her words, and ended his performance by nodding wisely. "I quite agree, dear lady. Something's going on around here that doesn't add up."

Annabel didn't know how she held her face together; she felt a twitch tugging at her lips, and knew that with very little provocation, she would succumb to

67

an outburst of giggles. None of which was in the least like her.

"I shall check the windows," Luke announced.

"And I shall telephone Jeremy," Aunt Marion decided.

Intervene now, dear, or prepare for a pajama party, Annabel's little voice suggested. "It was a spider," she improvised.

"Was it wearing clogs?" Luke asked, the devil incarnate laughing in his voice.

"Yes, Annabel," Marion hastened to offer. "We heard a lot of noise in here."

How had he managed it, Annabel wondered, amazed. He had the old dear convinced they'd arrived together, driven by mutual concern for her well-being. "It was a very large and ugly spider," she declared with feeling, looking Luke directly in the eye. "I threw a shoe at it—and missed."

Luke wasn't fazed. "You shouldn't have been so hard on him," he chided her. "Spiders do a lot of good, especially during the summer. They eat mosquitoes and get rid of other insect pests."

There was dire warning in his words.

CHAPTER FIVE

The following days were a waking nightmare for Annabel, made all the worse by the occasional glimpses of a paradise that wasn't hers to contemplate.

It began as early as the next morning. Everyone was seated when Annabel dragged herself down to breakfast. Sybil, her Cheshire cat grin barely under control, presided behind the heirloom silver coffee pot, and dispensed social chit-chat with an ease Annabel both loathed and envied. Next to her, Pandora scowled the length of the table to where Luke was cozied up next to Aunt Marion.

"Good morning, daughter mine," Sybil sang out in what Annabel perceived to be her mother's Blarney Stone voice. Sybil was in irrepressible high spirits and likely to be downright outrageous. Annabel was filled with foreboding.

"My dear, you look like the wrath of God," Aunt Marion piped up. "And no wonder. I was just telling your mother about last night."

"I think she looks radiant," Luke announced, passing over his cup to Sybil for refill. "What'll you have, Annabel? There's a feast over here on the buffet that would feed an army."

"Toast."

"Toast?"

Annabel glared at him. "You heard me. Toast."

Marion patted her mouth with her napkin and tapped Luke playfully on the arm. "Some of us have to watch our figures," she simpered. "We wouldn't want to be a fat bride, now would we?"

If there was one thing Annabel couldn't abide, it was the use of the royal "we." And second on her list of pet hates were women in their sixties who ignored the fact that they were long past their youthful prime, and carried on as if they were debutantes. "I see you're finished, Aunt Marion," she remarked, leaning over the lady's well-upholstered shoulder. "Let me take your plate for you, before I sit down."

"Allow me." Luke rose from the table, all six feet plus of casual elegance and charm. It made Annabel's teeth ache. "You sit and have a cup of your mother's excellent coffee, and I'll get your toast."

"And just a teeny helping of those marvelous grilled kidneys for me," Aunt Marion begged, wriggling with joy. "And perhaps a mushroom or two, and another rasher of bacon."

Annabel almost gagged.

Luke pulled out her chair for her. "Sit," he ordered.

"When I'm ready."

"Don't be cantankerous, Annabel," he murmured, placing a familiar hand in the small of her back and persuading her into place. "Things'll look better when you've got something solid inside you."

Solicitous words, but uttered with such evil intent, they made her blush.

"Breakfasts like these are almost a thing of the past," Marion lamented, attacking her food with relish, oblivious to the tensions and undercurrents swirling around.

"They're a family tradition with us. My father believed breakfast was the most important meal of the day," Sybil said, bestowing a fond gaze on Luke as she spoke, and releasing her Cheshire grin a fraction. Really, Annabel thought, her mother would've reached out and patted him on the head if her arms had been six inches longer.

"So true," Marion agreed between mouthfuls.

Settling himself next to Annabel, Luke propped a casual arm along the back of her chair and drew his coffee cup closer. "Tell us about him, Sybil," he invited, and Annabel heaved a sigh. The man was touched with genius. He knew precisely how to captivate women, regardless of their age; seemed possessed of the ability to reach them in their most vulnerable spots.

"My father," Sybil announced, her voice lilting with pleasure, "had a taste for living that I've never seen equaled. The family raised champion racehorses in Ireland, and some of my earliest memories are of going with him to the stables to see the newborn foals. He was as fine a judge of horseflesh as anyone, and an unparalleled connoisseur of beautiful women."

"Then his pride in his daughter must have taken precedence over all else," Luke said, and the smile he turned on her mother made Annabel's heart melt.

"I wish he'd lived to see his granddaughter. He'd have adored her." Sybil turned proud eyes on Annabel.

Luke's wonderful gray eyes followed, and Annabel felt the earth slipping away again. "Of course he would," he agreed, endearing himself to Sybil even

71

more. "How could he have helped it? How could anyone?"

"Why can't we have a dog?" Pandora, apparently tired of being ignored, flung out her question like a challenge.

"And what side of the family do you come from, dear boy?" Aunt Marion wanted to know, dismissing Pandora without so much as a blink. The question, and her daughter's unusual truculence, filled Annabel with apprehension. She sensed a storm was brewing.

"The wrong side, I'm afraid," Luke replied with such disarming candor that Marion dissolved into peals of merriment. "Would you like a dog, Pandora?"

Not about to be easily appeased, Pandora glowered at him. "I'm not allowed."

"You never before asked for one, dear heart," Sybil pointed out mildly. "There's no hard and fast rule that says you're not allowed."

Luke looked from Annabel to Sybil. "Then with your permission, maybe Pandora and I could spend some time together today, and that could be one of the things we'll discuss."

"I have school today," Pandora stated so baldly that Annabel found herself mouthing an apology for the child.

Luke dismissed her concern with a little shake of his head. "It's okay," he murmured. "She needs a little time, that's all. She's finding it tougher than she'd expected, now that I'm here in the flesh."

"I suppose," Pandora cut in, "that now that you're here, you've decided you don't like me."

"Not everyone likes children," Marion offered, at which Annabel quaked. She'd seen the desolate ex-

72

pression in her daughter's eyes, and recognized too well the umbrage that replaced it.

"Well, *he* should," Pandora insisted. "After all, he's supposed to be—"

"Related," Annabel gasped. "And not supposed, Pandora. He is, and you're excused."

Pandora flounced up from her chair. "What some people don't seem to realize is that not all *children* like grown-ups. I wish you hadn't bothered to come," she told Luke, her voice breaking. "It was better without you."

Marion opened her mouth wide to voice her opinion on such rudeness, then closed it again with a distinct clack of her dentures as she caught Sybil's forbidding eye on her.

Annabel was halfway along the terrace in pursuit of her daughter when Luke caught up with her. "Leave her, Annabel." His arms were inflexible, trapping her more firmly in the complexity of the web he was spinning about her.

"I can't! Look at what your coming here is doing to her. I've never seen her like this before."

He shook her gently. "I'm here because, whether you want to admit it or not, she felt she needed me. If something's tearing her apart now—and frankly, I think you're overreacting—it's more likely because you won't allow me to claim her as my daughter. You're so terrified she's going to open her mouth and call me 'Daddy' that you treated her at breakfast as if she weren't in the room. When she finally tried to get some attention, you hustled her off as if she had the plague."

"Well, isn't it wonderful? You come on the scene at

this late date and you're an instant expert on raising children. How did I manage without you till now?"

"I'm not sure," he replied, a smile lurking, "but now that I am here, let me try to help. You can't make someone the star of the show for ten years, then expect to shuffle them offstage when things get exciting. Pandora engineered this whole scene—with a little help from your mother—and she's not about to retire quietly to the wings now."

Annabel ground her teeth. Bad enough that he was right, without being reasonable too! "So what do we do next?"

He led her to a stone bench overlooking the shore below the garden. It was another beautiful June day. Wisteria hung in lavender clumps along the eaves of the house. Out to sea, sailboats cavorted in the light winds, almost as graceful as the gulls wheeling overhead. Across the gulf, a ferry picked its way through the low-lying islands drowsing in the lee of the big island.

Beautiful beyond imagining, until he looked again at Annabel, her hair curling around her face, her big blue-black eyes hiding behind the sweep of her lashes, her hands, long-fingered and elegant, clutched together. By comparison, the rest was just a setting—no less a backdrop than she deserved—and he felt an overriding urge to gather her in his arms and tell her exactly what they should do. Absurd though it might be, it seemed to him that here was a second chance at Eden, and they'd be fools to turn their backs on it again.

Disturbed, he let his gaze slide away. He couldn't look at her and maintain coherence or control. Something about her had him thinking one thing and saying another. The trouble was, he was increasingly unsure about which to believe: his mind, striving for logic, or his mouth spilling out feelings that, rooted in fantasy as they surely must be, nevertheless seemed perfectly valid.

Logic dictated that Pandora was the real cause of his turmoil. Even a man of his sanguine disposition was entitled to become a little flaky upon learning he had a ten-year-old daughter. It was natural enough, considering the bizarre turn of events, for everything else to shift out of focus in the light of this new discovery. Natural enough, too, that he should be so concerned about Annabel and the mistake he feared she was about to make. Her happiness, or lack of it, would affect those around her; specifically, his child.

So where did this ambivalence come from? Less, he sensed, from unsureness than from incredulity. He hadn't become a successful broker by hinging everything on certainty. He was, by nature and profession, something of a gambler, and never one to run away from a challenge. But he was used to dealing with tangibles: profit and loss, dollars and cents; speculation and blue chip investments. Concrete concepts, defined in the black and white of market analyses. Nothing about his feelings for Annabel could be summarized in a report; they defied analysis.

One of the joys of reaching forty, he'd discovered, was the courage to trust his instincts. In the normal order of things, he'd follow them without a qualm. But this time, his was not the only life to be affected, should they be wrong. Two other people stood to lose as well, and that was where the doubt crept in. Did he really have the right to disrupt their lives, on the strength of a hunch that he'd find more happiness with

Annabel than he'd ever dared to hope for? Or should he stick to the simpler issue: deal with the child, and let the man who wanted the job have Annabel. *But which man was that?*

Sitting on his hands because he was afraid of what they might do if he didn't, he hunched his shoulders and concentrated on the city skyline, spread out to the northeast. "I think you must decide what to do next, Annabel," he said quietly, "because if it's left to me, I'll suggest something that'll either upset or offend you."

"But I need you . . . to help me."

Oh, what that hesitation in her words did to him! All the hazy fragments that were his memories of her reassembled, a movie in reverse. The infatuation of their time together in Maui resurfaced, welded by a deeper bond that defied reason. Was it just history, gilded by time to seem better than it really was? Or something more?

Enough of the pipe dreams. "Look, Annabel," he began, full of brotherly good sense that he didn't expose to ridicule by risking another look at her, "you must surely know that Jeremy will find out about me eventually. So what? It's not as if you're springing a daughter on him at the last minute. He already knows about Pandora, and has, presumably, accepted her."

Annabel gave a little whimper of distress, but he hardened his heart. "For crying out loud, he's a doctor. He knows you didn't pick up a baby at the supermarket, lodged alphabetically between asparagus and cabbage, you foolish girl."

His words destroyed her. "I'll have you know," she replied, anger struggling to overlay the pain that trembled in her voice, "that I ceased to be a girl the day I

76

found out I was expecting your child, though foolish I undoubtedly must still be, to let you unsettle me like this."

"Unsettle, darling?" His ear had caught something that gave away more than she realized. It wasn't just his imagination. There was something between him and this woman that had nothing at all to do with the child they shared. "How have I done that?"

"You make me wish—"

He turned to look at her again. He couldn't help himself. He savored all of her: her mouth all pouting and soft; her big, beautiful eyes that reminded him of twilight in summer; the perfect loveliness of her face. Even more, he looked into her, sank inside her, and discovered something exquisite and fragile that was in danger of dying. And in that moment, he knew he'd go to any lengths, climb any number of mountains, to make it come alive again. At her stricken expression, he reached out and captured her hands. "What, Annabel? What do I make you wish?"

"That you'd stayed away." But her fingers were clinging to him, almost as much as her eyes. "Everything would have stayed the same, if only you hadn't come."

"Nothing stays the same forever."

He straddled the bench, haloed in early-morning sunlight, dangerously attractive. She'd heard him say he was a stockbroker, a man whose profession dictated the ultraconservative business suit of last night, but this morning, his dimensions and inclinations conformed to the soft and weathered texture of suede and denim, reviving echoes of that young man who'd stolen her heart along with her innocence.

It was a lethal combination. There was such gentleness in his voice, such ardor in his gaze, that she feared herself half in love with him already, astonished and helpless to find that he'd taken possession of her again, so soon. "I don't want changes," she whispered, panic-stricken. "I want things to stay the same —safe and uncomplicated. I was happy until you came back. I had the rest of my life under control. It isn't fair of you to make it all seem so empty. Go away and leave me in peace."

"Darling Annabel, what about desire? Romance? What about the driving hunger to possess, and be possessed, by another?"

Oh no, not that! Never again. That was what had brought on all her heartbreak before. "I don't need it. I just want a nice, comfortable marriage."

He disengaged her hands, filling her with the desolate hope that he'd accept what she'd told him, but he wasn't about to be so easily put off. "Really?" He imprisoned her face in his two hands, and no amount of determination could release her fascinated gaze from his mouth as it inched toward hers. "Are you sure?"

He filled her senses, the smell of him laced with sunlight and summer, the sight of him, tall and tanned, eclipsing the image of the man who should have been able to exorcise him. And then, at last, the feel of him: his mouth warm and compelling on hers, and his hands, strong and urgent, sliding down her jaw and around her neck. All of him so breathtaking, he made her want to cast out all her private fears and dare to live again.

"I don't think you're very sure at all, Annabel." His breathing was that of a man who'd run a mile uphill in record time. "I think you're lying again."

"Think what you like," she murmured faintly, and on an impulse that she later had to admit was purely insane, coiled her arms around his neck and initiated another kiss that laid bare all the untruths she'd been telling herself for years. She didn't need this; she craved it.

But it was a stolen moment, one she couldn't keep. Whatever her heart might be trying to tell her, her life was too closely interwoven with Jeremy's for her to break free now. She had made a commitment to him, and she'd known from the start that it had more to do with companionship than passion; with contentment than with ecstasy. Love was blatant and autocratic, whereas affection lent itself to discretion, touching a person's life with gladness and leaving the heart intact.

If the price of such restraint now seemed too high, all she had to do was remember how dearly its absence had cost her before. Everyone else might have forgiven her for flouting convention and bearing a child out of wedlock; she might even have forgiven herself, but she had never forgotten the utter anguish of allowing her emotions free rein.

She'd never known want of any kind until then. She'd taken for granted the wealth and social prominence to which she'd been born but which she'd done nothing to earn. At eighteen, she'd been one of the beautiful people, and never questioned her right to be so. At nineteen, she'd learned two lessons that were to remain with her: not even the beautiful people are immune to heartbreak, and worse, they are objects of unending speculation and comment when they fall from their high perch.

Knowing that her fine family name was being bandied about the cocktail circuit, at the mercy of the gossip that filtered its way into the society pages of the local papers, was something for which she'd never forgiven herself. It wasn't a mistake she was about to repeat by jilting one of the city's most respected and prestigious surgeons for a man she barely knew. The scandalmongers would sniff out the truth, and once again have a field day at her family's expense.

Which was why she put everything she had to offer in that one last kiss: all the giving and all the taking of which she was capable. And all the pain. It might have been her last day on earth, so fervently did she cling to him. She imprinted the memory of him on her soul—how he tasted, how he felt—as if she wanted to take a little bit of him with her into eternity.

Luke ended the kiss much too soon. "Oh, my darling girl," he muttered, pulling her even closer and burying his lips in her hair, "what have you started?"

"Nothing." All her potential for joy seemed to shred into pieces, leaving her so ragged and incomplete that she didn't know how she'd ever go on. "I just ended something."

"What?"

"Us. You and me. Whatever it is that makes us behave as if there's something special between us."

He gaped at her. "You kiss me like that, then try to tell me there isn't?"

"Nothing of substance. You're looking for the Annabel you once knew, but she's grown up now, and one of the things she's learned is that wishing doesn't make it so."

He let go of her, his expression bleak. In a futile gesture of comfort, she reached up and replaced a strand of hair that had fallen over his brow. "I wish so many things," she whispered. "That we'd fallen in love and married and raised Pandora together; that we'd met under different circumstances, and dated, the way kids do—that you'd sent me flowers, and Valentine cards, and been my escort at graduation."

Was this the same woman who claimed not to need romance or passion? "It's not too late—"

"It is too late. I'm going to marry another man, and he's too good and honorable to be treated so shabbily."

"Let me be good and honorable." Let me cut out my heart for you. Let me love you. *Let yourself love me*.

Shattered, for he had no recollection ever of begging a woman for anything, he closed his eyes. When Melinda had told him she was leaving, he'd opened the door to speed her on her way, relieved at the freedom he was gaining and not once regretting it in the years that followed. But now, with Annabel, he wanted to make impossible promises, to atone for his ignorance and omissions of yesterday, and to be the one to make all her tomorrows beautiful.

"It's too late for us, Luke."

It was the first time she'd spoken his name with anything approaching tenderness. It almost undid him. "Not for me, it isn't."

She couldn't bear the grief that darkened his eyes to slate and, in an effort to lessen it, offered to share with him the dearest thing she possessed—the one thing she'd most feared he'd try to take away from her last night. How quickly things changed. "You're right. It's not too late for you and Pandora. She's your daughter and nothing will ever change that. Get to know her and learn to love her."

"I'll do that without your permission," he informed

81

her harshly, "but don't expect me to make her a substitute for you. That's not how it works."

"She can fill your life with pleasure, the way she has mine."

He inhaled a great sigh and gripped the sides of the bench with hands that looked more capable of throttling than caressing her. "For a bright woman, you come out with some cockamamie ideas. Parents, dear Annie, have no right to make their children the repository of all their hopes and dreams. Our happiness is not their responsibility. Pandora has her own visions. Neither you nor I have the right to inflict her with ours."

She recoiled as though he'd slapped her. "And that's what you think I'm doing?"

"It's what you've done, and now, having seen the error of your ways, you're making a gesture of independence. Except that's all it is, Annie—an empty gesture. Pandora's smart beyond her years, and she knows exactly why you're marrying Jeremy. And if you think she's not carrying a load of guilt about that, then think again."

"Just what did she say in that letter?"

"That's my business and hers. If she wants you to know, she'll tell you herself. But I will tell you this, sweet face: you're screwing up all around with this marriage of yours. The way you're going about it, no one's going to come out a winner, least of all the poor slob you've selected for a husband."

To think she'd entertained, even briefly, the idea that she could love this man! "Let me see the letter."

"Not a chance." It afforded him immeasurable satisfaction to see her distress match his own.

"Suit yourself. My mind's made up, anyway, and

even if it weren't, it's too late to change things now. Arrangements have been made, I have a social obligation—"

"Arrangements? Social obligations?" They might have been obscenities, the way he mouthed them. "You'd hinge your future on that sort of crap?"

"People like us," she began, but he cut her off with a blistering oath.

"People like you," he sneered, "strike me as being a few bales short of a full load of hay. The perfectly proper Ms. Pryce intends to become the excruciatingly correct Mrs. Carson, come hell or high water."

Annabel rose to her feet. This had gone on long enough and was achieving nothing. "I think I will leave now," she declared, with the utmost dignity. "I have a class to teach at eleven."

"And I think I'll go and throw up," Luke shot back, leaping to his feet and taking off down the steps that led to the beach as though he found her company unendurable.

Sybil joined him at the water's edge half an hour later.

"I'm lousy company," he warned her.

"So I gather from the way you're beetling your brows at me." Undeterred, she slipped an arm through his. "Still and all, I hope you'll adjust your stride. My sprinting days are over."

He didn't think he had it in him to grin, but one formed anyway, and slipped out before he could contain it. "You're a remarkable woman, Sybil, and I'd rather die than cause you any more grief than I already have, but I've got to tell you, I could strangle that daughter of yours."

"Oh, leave that as a last resort," she replied comfortably. "What do you mean: cause me any more grief than you already have?"

"Well, I'm the one who got Annabel pregnant when she was barely out of high school."

"My dear young man, Pandora is a source of unending pleasure to me. You should be proud. She has very fine genes, and some of them are yours." She stopped and looked up at him. "Are you upset by her behavior at breakfast?"

"Not a bit. As Annabel was so quick to point out, I'm no expert on children, but from what I've observed, they seem to get over their moods pretty fast. She'll come around, I'm sure."

"Bless us all, the man's got brains as well as looks! Now tell me, what do you plan to do about our Annabel?"

Luke thrust his hands into the pockets of his jeans and stared moodily out to sea. "The way I see it, Sybil, there's not much I can do. Our Annabel's got her face all set on marrying the good doctor."

"You disappoint me, Luke. I hadn't expected you to throw in the towel quite so soon, especially not after the way you were kissing her out there on the terrace."

Hope surged in him. If Annabel had talked to Sybil about that, maybe her mind wasn't as made up as she'd have him believe. "How'd you find out?"

"I was spying on you from the upstairs landing window."

He must have looked as crestfallen as he felt, because before he could utter a word, she continued: "It seems to me you've made extraordinary progress. Not yet here twenty-four hours and already you're igniting her in a way she's never known before—at least, not since she first met you."

"That's nice to hear, Sybil, but not exactly the way it is. She's made it pretty clear she doesn't want me fouling things up, and I have to accept that she knows what she's talking about."

"Poppycock! Annabel can be obtuse, to put it mildly. In anyone else's child, I'd go so far as to call it outright stupidity. You mustn't listen to what she *says,* dear. Remember the old adage: actions speak louder than words. Sit back for a day or so, and observe. Spend some time with your daughter. Then, if you still feel the same way . . . well, then we'll have to have another little chat, and I'll pour more unasked-for advice in your ear."

She reached into the pocket of her linen pants and popped a pair of sunglasses on her nose. "Oh, I do relish the prospect of being a mother-in-law. It presents such opportunities to meddle!"

He heard his laughter explode before he realized she'd dispelled almost all his gloom. "Then maybe you shouldn't encourage me to disrupt her wedding plans."

"It's not the wedding plans I'm objecting to, so much as the choice of groom. Jeremy is far too nice to be served up like cold leftovers. You, however, strike me as something of a rogue. You deserve Annabel."

"I'll try not to disappoint you."

"Try very hard, Luke, or I'll be having to take matters into my own hands. By the way, Jeremy's coming for dinner tomorrow night. Don't plan to be discreet and disappear for the evening, will you?"

"I wouldn't dream of it."

Sybil smiled, and it struck him how very much she reminded him of the cat from *Alice in Wonderland.*

CHAPTER SIX

Something happened at the hospital that day that gave Annabel pause. She stayed later than usual in the office she shared with two other instructors because she couldn't face going home and dealing with Luke. By doing so, she overheard a conversation among a group of nursing students that was never meant for her ears.

"I failed the final," a voice announced miserably.

"You had reasons," another consoled. "Getting dumped by the man you thought you were going to marry is enough to make anyone blow an exam. Go tell Pryce what happened. She'll probably let you write a makeup test."

"Don't count on it," a third voice commented. "Remember how upset I was when my folks had to have my dog put down? I bawled my eyes out all over a patient who'd had a simple appendectomy, and was going home that day. Pryce caught me at it and told me a good nurse learned not to let her emotions interfere with her work."

Annabel's mouth fell open. She wanted to run out into the hall and tell the girl: But I didn't know your dog had died!

Of course you didn't, dear, her little voice piped up. *You make a point of keeping your distance from everyone. You didn't even know your own daughter wanted a dog, for Pete's sake!*

"Maybe she doesn't like dogs . . ."

I do, I do!

"But you'd think she'd be more understanding about this. After all, she's engaged herself."

"And tickled pink by it, if the look on her face today was any indication," number two chimed in. "I tell you, if I'd snagged a man like Dr. Carson, you couldn't keep the grin off my face."

"Well, let's be honest, Denise," someone else laughed, "you came into nursing with the express intention of catching a rich doctor. You're just jealous because Little Annie Fanny beat you to it."

Little Annie Fanny?

"I just hate to see such a good man go to waste," number two replied, giggling like a fourteen-year-old. "I mean, why's she doing it, if she finds it all such a drag? I've seen them in the cafeteria together. She looks at him the way I look at oatmeal—good for what ails you, but dull."

"She's got a child somewhere, hasn't she? Perhaps that's got something to do with it."

"Maybe I'm the lucky one," the first voice sniffed. "I'd rather not be married at all than be tolerated for the sake of convenience. Marriage is tough enough, if my parents are any example, without going into it for the wrong reasons."

"Hey," another suggested, "for some folks, a bad marriage is better than no marriage at all."

By a supreme effort, Annabel restrained herself from rushing out into the hall and telling the lot of them that they were too wet behind the ears to have the faintest idea what they were talking about. Only the suspicion that they might be right kept her inside the office, and silent.

"Jeremy baby deserves better," the voluble Denise retorted, her fount of wisdom apparently far from exhausted. "She should leave him for someone who'll appreciate him—like me."

. . . no one's going to come out a winner, least of all the poor slob you've selected for a husband . . . Luke's words echoed in Annabel's head, taunting her afresh.

Fishing her car keys out of her purse, she opened the door and stepped out into the hall, prepared to confront her latest critics, confident that she could silence them a lot more easily than she could Luke. But the hallway had emptied.

What do they know, anyway? she thought. *They're just babies.*

They're the same age you were, dearie, when you gave birth to Pandora. Pity you didn't have half their savvy. Maybe then you wouldn't be in such a pickle now.

Shut up! Annabel told the despicable little voice. You're supposed to be on my side. Someone has to be, for God's sake!

And someone was, now that she thought about it. Jeremy, for instance, and his mother. When she'd met Barbara Carson for lunch that day, they'd had a nice little chat about the wedding, and Mrs. Carson had said how pleased she was that Jeremy had finally decided to settle down.

"He's devoted such a lot of time to medicine, Annabel, that he never felt he could afford to develop a serious relationship until now," Mrs. Carson had said. "How fortunate that you met when you did."

And how convenient, for both of them. Caught in the rush-hour traffic by her late departure from work,

Annabel found herself whiling away the time by re-living the rest of the conversation she'd had with her future mother-in-law, and it was more than the sun slanting across the windshield that caused the pucker between her eyes.

"Thank goodness you're so mature," Mrs. Carson had continued. "A doctor's work always comes first, but you understand that he needs a wife to come home to at the end of the day—or night, as the case may be—who won't make unreasonable demands on him. And then, of course, he does have a certain social status to maintain, and the right kind of wife certainly makes it easier to achieve."

Undeniably, a most sensible arrangement.

"It took me a long time to accept that with Jeremy's father," Barbara Carson had concluded, fingering the pearls that nestled among the white lace ruffles of her blouse, "but you're much wiser than I was."

It had been intended as a compliment, she was sure, but now that she'd had time to digest it, Annabel wasn't sure she wanted to be quite that understanding. Perhaps because of what she'd overheard outside her office, it struck her that she didn't care for the picture of her that Mrs. Carson had painted.

"Mature" left her feeling she was over the hill, and as for "wise"—well, it smacked too much of "unimagi-native" to suit Annabel. By her own admission, Barbara Carson had been none of those things when she was younger, but it didn't prevent her husband from looking at her today as if she were the sugarplum fairy, delectable enough to eat, and pure pleasure to look at.

Annabel had the feeling that it wasn't Barbara's wis-dom, or her talents as a society hostess, that put the gleam in the senior Carson's eye. A gleam, now that she thought about it, that was noticeably absent from the glances his son bestowed on his intended bride.

"I know! I'm getting what I contracted for," Annabel told the interior of the car, before the little voice could say it for her, "but I think I'd like to be something more than a housekeeper with privileges, and I know just where I'm going to begin to make the change."

With unusual flair and a great squealing of tires, she shot ahead into the passing lane and made an illegal left turn that would lead her back into town. "Hey, lady," the affronted driver of the car behind yelled after her, "take a taxi and keep death off the roads, huh?"

Annabel blew him a kiss in her rearview mirror—another uncharacteristic gesture—and earned an exasperated wave before she became swallowed up in the traffic heading the other way.

Pandora attended an exclusive private school which insisted its pupils wear snazzy little uniforms, Luke discovered, and wondered if his decision to meet his daughter after class was such a bright idea. He wasn't sure he'd recognize her in the sudden outpouring into the parking lot of gray flannel skirts and scarlet jackets, but nor did he feel up to going inside the building and asking for help. They'd probably think he was some kind of pervert since he had neither ID nor anything else that established his right to cart one of their precious charges away. Furthermore, he felt decidedly uneasy in the midst of so many small people.

They came in all shapes and sizes at this place, and swarmed around him like so many bees, each one intent on finding its own hive. Car doors opened and closed with well-mannered clicks, as mothers with expensive smiles greeted their offspring. Belatedly, he realized he was the only male in sight.

"Excuse me," a passing munchkin informed him, in that odd West Coast accent that he found so attractive in Annabel, "but your car is parked in the fire lane, and Mrs. MacDermott will have it towed if you don't move it."

He looked down at the small face peering up at his. "I didn't see the sign," he apologized and, with enormous relief, saw Pandora coming toward him.

He should have known better than to expect her to be pleased to see him. "Hey," she parroted, "you're in—"

"The fire lane. Yes, I know. I didn't see the sign."

Pandora went around the other side of the car and climbed in. "How could anyone miss it?" she inquired of the maple trees that bordered the area.

How indeed, twit? he admonished himself. Try to do something right for a change, can't you?

"Grandmother must like you," Pandora offered, as he backed out of the parking lot and merged with the traffic. "She doesn't let just anyone drive her car."

"Maybe she sees something in me that you've missed."

There was a silence that lasted for a number of blocks, during which time Luke concluded that he wasn't cut out for fatherhood. He had no idea how to start a conversation with this person who happened, by accident, to be his daughter.

Whistling between his teeth, he concentrated on transporting her back to the house as speedily as safety would allow, after which he intended to stretch out on the terrace with a beer, and contemplate a future without Annabel. All things considered, the Pryce women terrified him.

"Actually, you're a pretty good driver," Pandora conceded. "I don't suppose you'd teach me how?"

"Where I come from, the driving age is sixteen," he told her.

"Well, I know that." She looked at him as though he'd undergone a lobotomy that hadn't worked, and in her expression, he saw something that reminded him of himself at that age. Maybe they could communicate after all. "But that's only six years away," she reasoned. "Or aren't you planning to be around then?"

"It sort of depends on you, Pandora. Do you think you'd like to have me around?"

She looked at him with the judicious air of one appraising an antique of dubious authenticity. "Maybe."

It was ridiculous to feel so warmed by her qualified acceptance. "I think maybe I'd like that, too."

"How can you tell? You don't know anything about me."

"I know as much about you as you know about me."

"No. I know more," she insisted mysteriously.

"Yeah," he agreed, "I guess you do." They were almost at the house, and he wished that weren't so. They'd only just started to make any headway in this father-child business.

"Well?" she prompted.

"Well what?"

"Don't you want to know what I know?"

Since anything she knew would have been related to her by Annabel, he wasn't sure he did. On the other hand, he could hardly defend himself if he remained in the dark. "What say we go for a little drive," he suggested, "and you can tell me what you think you know, and I'll tell you if you're right."

"We'd better. We're not getting anywhere right now."

How perceptive she was, and how daunting! "Sort of like elephants walking around in a circle, holding on to each other's tails."

She giggled, a startling enough sound from so solemn a child, that he looked around to make sure she was responsible for it. Her face, all scrunched up with the effort not to laugh outright, charmed him. For the first time, she was acting her age, instead of ten going on forty. "Okay, where to?"

"The park," she decided. "It has swings."

Good God, he thought, she'll probably make hers go higher than mine, and I'll be back to square one: the guy who didn't live up to her expectations.

They were there in minutes. "So," he began, locking up the car, "what do you know about me?"

"That you didn't wear glasses till you grew old." She skipped along beside him, oblivious of the blow to his pride. "And that you took advantage of my mother in a storm."

"Huh?"

"I'm not sure what that means," she confided blithely. "I asked mommy, and she said you weren't a gentleman, so I suppose you didn't let her use your umbrella, or something."

"I let her share my cabin until the storm ended, and I kept her warm and dry." And never mind how, kiddo. Get the details from your mother, since she's so free with her information, and let's see her wriggle out of that one.

"Also," Pandora went on, really getting into stride

now, "you have a hairy chest and hairy legs, and you turn brown in the sun, and mommy doesn't. Nor do I," she informed him dolefully, then on a more cheerful note: "but I don't have a hairy chest, either."

"Well, thank God for that." It would have been his fault for sure, if she had.

"You met each other in Maui—I've been there, but we didn't stay in the same place, because mommy said it brought things back—and after, you went your way, and she went hers, and if my grandfather had been alive, he'd have come after you with a shotgun." She drew in an important breath and dealt the coup de grace: "In fact, you were a bit of a cattle ear."

"I beg your pardon?"

"A cattle ear."

"That's what I thought you said." The metaphor left him puzzled, though he guessed there were less flattering parts of a cow to which he could have been likened. "I don't suppose you know what that means, either?"

"Of course I do," she said, rolling her eyes, and hopping around him like an eager frog. "I asked Grandmother, and she said it meant you were 'a silver-tongued charmer.' "

He laughed, comprehension dawning. "Ah! A bit of a *cavalier*."

"That's what I said. Also," she rushed on, when he opened his mouth to defend himself, "you were a hippie and had long hair."

"And you, miss, are lippy. You're almost as saucy as your mother was when I first met her." He narrowed his eyes at her. "Did she really tell you I had a hairy chest and legs?"

Pandora looked shocked. "Oh no," she assured

94

him. "She didn't tell me any of the good stuff. She told me that you were a nice man, and that if you'd known about me, you'd have loved me."

There was a pregnant silence which Luke felt compelled to fill. "Um . . . yes . . . I'm sure I would have."

"Well? Now that you have, do you?"

Oh, Jeez! "I'm thinking about it."

"You don't have long to make up your mind. The wedding's next week."

"My loving you has nothing to do with the wedding. You're my daughter, no matter who your mother marries."

"But she's marrying Jeremy so I grow up normal."

"She says that has nothing to do with it, and anyway, you are far above being merely normal. You're the most extraordinary person of your age I've ever known."

"So if you do decide to love me," Pandora, with a courage he admired, pursued the topic relentlessly, "it won't be because you feel you have to."

If she'd been this insistent on truth all her life, he felt sorry for Annabel and Sybil. What could he say to her? Of course he felt an obligation. He wished he didn't. And he wished he could answer her question with as much candor as she'd asked it. "You know something, Pandora? I think this is a major event in our lives, and we should take it a day at a time for, say, the next five days. I mean, what if I decide I want everyone to know who I really am? What if I ask you to call me 'dad' or 'father' or 'pops'—"

She burst out with another giggle. "Or 'pappy' or 'Daddy Warbucks' or—"

"Right. And what if you've decided by then that you

95

want me to go away and never bother you again? I mean, I've got feelings, too, you know."

"I don't think I'll do that."

"But you don't know—that's my whole point. So why don't we spend the next five days getting to know all about each other, and then call a conference."

"A private conference."

"Very private, just between you and me."

"Like a secret society."

"Exactly. We won't tell anyone else who I really am. In fact, you'd better call me Luke until you decide if you want anyone else to know I'm really your father." Keeping his identity under wraps for a few days would suit Annabel.

Pandora looked doubtful. "I don't know . . . what about Uncle Luke? I'm not supposed to call older people by their first names. Mommy says it's not re-spectful."

"No 'uncle'!" He was her father, dammit, and not about to be demoted. "And it's okay to use first names if the older person gives you permission. And while we're on the subject, I'm not exactly in my dotage, you know."

"What's a dotage?"

"Ready for retirement."

"But you've got lots of gray hair."

And likely to get plenty more, at this rate. "Never mind. Tell me something: if you didn't learn every-thing about me from your mother, how did you find it out?"

"I listen a lot. People forget that children have ears, you know."

Not this joker, Luke decided. I'll watch every sylla-ble from here on in. "She talks about me that much?"

"No, and only to grandmother."

"She told your grandmother I had a hairy chest?"

Pandora hooted with merriment, and made a bee-line for the swings. "I found that out all by myself. Push me."

"Please—and only if you tell me how you found out." He hauled back on the chains and held her suspended, with her skinny little legs sticking out in front of her.

"I've seen your picture," she squealed, full of terrified glee. "Let me go. I'm slipping off the seat and I'll get slivers in my bottom."

"Heaven forbid!" He released her, and sent her soaring in a great billow of gray flannel. He wasn't having slivers in his daughter's behind. "What picture?"

"One of you that mommy took in Maui. You were wearing shorts and thongs on the beach, and your hair was blowing all over the place."

The vague memory of their last morning together filtered back to him. The ocean was still in an uproar, and the trades still blowing like gales, but the rain had stopped and the skies cleared. Later that day, the phones had been restored, and he'd confirmed his flight back to Toronto, too full of guilt at his infidelity to spare a thought for what Annabel might have been feeling, or even to consider what the last three days had really meant to him. "She has a picture?" How did Jeremy feel about that?

"Yes, but she doesn't know I've seen it. She keeps it in her drawer with her underwear."

Did she, indeed. How delightfully erotic! "So how did you know it was me?"

97

"Because she wrote on the back—your name, and the date and the place."

"But not my address, so how did you know where to find me?"

"Grandmother helped me. She said you were quite well known in business circles, and it was easy to find out where you worked. She said it was okay to write to your office, but that sending a letter to your house might be embarrassing."

"How so?"

"In case you were married, or something." She gave a little squeal and dragged her feet in the sandy dirt, jarring herself to a halt. "Are you?"

"No." He occupied the swing next to hers and hooked his arms around the chains, rocking gently by scuffing his feet back and forth. They had the park to themselves, and he knew the most extraordinary sense of contentment. Somewhere out of sight, water trickled over stones and splashed into a hidden pool, and the late-afternoon sunshine profiled the trailing branches of a weeping willow in gold.

"And do you have any other children?"

"None that I know of."

"Well, you didn't know about me, either," she pointed out, not missing a trick, "so maybe I've got a dozen brothers and sisters somewhere."

Outmaneuvered again! He could barely contain his hilarity. "I doubt that. I'm sure I'd have heard if I had. Not every woman's as proud and close-mouthed as your mother."

It struck him that this was a very adult sort of topic to be discussing with his daughter, and wondered what Annabel would have to say, should she hear about it.

"Or as stubborn. Do you think you can stop the wedding?"

She was scuffing her feet and had looped her arms around the chains of her swing, just like him. She seemed very much at ease, but her little face, he noticed, was tight with anxiety. "I don't know that I have the right to try."

"Well but . . . why do you think I wrote the letter? Mommy's getting married because she thinks I should know what it's like to have a father, not because she really loves Jeremy."

The way she said "loves" was so intense that Luke knew she, too, saw as clearly as he, how Annabel was shortchanging herself.

"If you decide really to be my father," Pandora finished slyly, "then she wouldn't have any reason to get married."

"I think she'd like to be married."

"Then she could marry you, and I'd have my real mother and father both at the same time."

"What have you got against Jeremy?"

"Well, he's very boring, although he tries to be fun. He looks younger than you, but he acts even older. I think you'd be better for Mommy."

Remarkable, he thought, how alike their minds were in this respect. Unrealistic, too, but she could be forgiven for oversimplifying such a complex issue, whereas he knew better. "But she doesn't really *love* me, either, Pandora. In fact, I'm not sure she even likes me very much."

"So what?" she countered with single-minded logic. "If she wants me to have a father and she's going to get married anyway, she might as well go for the real thing."

Wouldn't it be nice, he reflected, to be able to indulge in such unashamed selfishness? If he and Annabel had been less concerned with other people and more intent on themselves, who was to say where their relationship might not have gone, all those years ago. They could have been married for over a decade, and have three more like Pandora.

A cold sweat brought him hurriedly to his feet. He had his hands full coping with one child. "We'd better think about heading back, cupcake. You probably have homework."

"No." She trotted to catch up with him and slipped her hand confidingly in his, reviving all his preposterous daydreams. He could get used to fatherhood, no doubt about it. He could get used to marriage, too. Particularly if it involved Annabel. "There's only two more days of school left till summer vacation."

He found himself making plans that would never have occurred to him two days ago.

The car keys were nowhere to be found. "Ah, shee —oot!" Just in time, he remembered his daughter's penchant for overhearing things not suited to her ears

She was looking at him, saucer-eyed with fascination. "Is that a swear word?"

"Not really."

"Oh. Have you lost the keys?"

"It's beginning to look that way. Well . . ." He gave his pockets a final slap, ". . . I guess we'll have to backtrack and try to find them."

The keys were at the swings, but they'd been covered with sand from where he'd dragged his feet back and forth. He was just about ready to give up and go find a phone when Pandora, who'd been scrabbling around in the dirt, located them, half an hour later.

"Nice going, Panda-Bear." He took them from her grubby little paw. "We'd better hit the road, before they send out a search party."

But it was too late to avoid Annabel's wrath. She was waiting at the house, and she was not happy.

"Where have you been with my daughter?" she demanded, and then, before he could answer, went on, incensed: "Look at the toes of her shoes, all scuffed up. And she's filthy! What were you doing, rolling around in the dirt?"

"We went to the park, Mommy."

"The park? You took her to the park, without asking me first?"

"I'm her father, Annabel, not the local pervert. What's wrong with taking her to the park?"

"Don't talk like that in front of her!"

Pandora rushed in to try to save the day. "It's okay, Mom, I know all about those things. We went there to be private. We had things to talk about," she added, darkly.

Annabel bristled with suspicion. "Such as?"

"None of your business," he told her. "Just be glad we came home when we did. We were having such a good time, we could have stayed out all night."

"And I could have you arrested for kidnapping."

"Oh, for Christ's sake, Annabel!" He flung up both hands in exasperation. "Don't be so damn silly."

"Yes, Mommy." Pandora flung up her hands, too, like a well-trained chimpanzee. "Shee—oot, you're no fun at all."

Annabel turned pale, then blushed most becomingly. Luke was practically in stitches at Pandora's behavior, but he quickly put a damper on his merriment when he realized how enraged Annabel was.

He'd often wondered if he'd know a virago if he saw one. He learned in the next five minutes that he would. He also learned, in short order, that Annabel disapproved of bad language, didn't appreciate backtalk from tardy ten-year-olds, and after Pandora had been sent to wash up for dinner, that he needed a keeper and wasn't fit to be let out in polite society.

He tried to look suitably contrite, but it was difficult when Annabel was so fiery and magnificently uninhibited. If she were his woman, he thought, he'd make her angry more often, just for the sheer pleasure of watching that Irish temper overcome all that Russian reserve.

CHAPTER SEVEN

The next morning Annabel awoke dreading that evening's dinner party. She couldn't bear thinking of sitting between Luke and Jeremy at dinner. In fact, she couldn't bear seeing any of them. For that reason, she decided to absent herself for most of the day.

Her daughter's father was a most disruptive presence, and she had other things to do besides waste valuable time trying to counteract his influence on Pandora. The child had been unmanageable last night, and Annabel was furious at Luke for creating such a ridiculous scene. She wasn't given to hysterical outbursts, and the memory of her own behavior was an even greater embarrassment than Pandora's. Just thinking about it put a scowl on her face that would have soured milk.

Of course, he was there at the breakfast table again, his chair so close to Pandora's that the two of them were practically sitting in each other's laps.

"Good morning, sunshine." He smiled at her, the epitome of good humor.

"Good morning, Mommy," Pandora echoed, her face suffused with amusement—a rather rare occurrence for her.

Irritated though she was, Annabel couldn't help but

notice how much they resembled each other, the man and the child, and it was an effect brought about as much by the animation in their faces as by any specific feature. It dismayed her to realize that, on top of everything else, she was jealous—again.

"What can we get for you? Coffee? Toast?"

Honestly, anyone would think this was his house, and she the guest. "If I needed a servant, Luke, I'd hire one." She stalked to the buffet and selected a piece of fruit. "As it is, I'm perfectly capable of looking after myself. Good morning, Mother."

"Sit down, Annabel."

"No thanks. It's too beautiful a morning to sit in here. I'll take my coffee out to the terrace."

"What are your plans for today?" Sybil wore her Cheshire face again, and from its expression, she might have swallowed a quart of cream.

"I have some shopping to do." Her secret mission of yesterday was not complete, and time was running short.

Luke looked up. "Feel like some company, Annabel? I wouldn't mind seeing something of downtown. There's a rumor down east that Vancouver is one beautiful city."

"Sorry," she replied, her tone anything but apologetic. "I'm getting married in a few days. I don't have time to play tour guide." She picked up her cup and swept outside before he could formulate any response.

Sybil joined her there a few minutes later. "Annabel, you aren't being very charming to our guest."

"He's your guest, Mother. You invited him to stay here. You be charming."

"Well," Sybil replied modestly, "I always am, but it wouldn't hurt you to make some effort, too."

"After last night, I don't feel inclined to do anything but ignore him."

"I'm sure he didn't lose the keys on purpose, and in any case, there was no harm done."

"He's undermining my authority with Pandora. She would never have dreamed of speaking to me that way —or using that kind of language—a week ago."

"Don't be making something out of nothing, my darling. And don't frown that way. You'll give yourself lines."

Annabel jumped to her feet. "This is all your fault, you know, Mother. If you hadn't encouraged Pandora to get in touch with him, everything would still be going smoothly. I hope you're happy with your handiwork."

"Are you telling me, dear heart, that things are not going smoothly now? And if not, may I ask what has changed?" Sybil, to Annabel's annoyance, couldn't subdue the anticipation in her voice.

"Well, I'm not having second thoughts about marrying Jeremy, if that's what you're hoping, but if Pandora becomes totally obnoxious, you can consider yourself as much to blame as her father. There'd better be no more interference from you, Mother."

"Ha," Sybil muttered into her coffee cup, "I'm only just getting into stride."

"You're talking to yourself again, Mother. You know how that annoys me."

"Dear child," Sybil ad-libbed, "all I was doing was reminding myself: you're going to be a bride. We must make allowances for you. Why don't you pamper yourself while you're out, and have a facial or something?"

"Am I still going to be a bridesmaid?" Pandora, Luke at her side, appeared from the dining room.

"Were you eavesdropping?" Annabel demanded, irritated afresh by the sight of Pandora clutching Luke by the hand as if she feared he might drop off the edge of the earth.

"What a suspicious mind you have, Annie," Luke chided her. "Of course she wasn't eavesdropping. We thought we'd take a walk along the beach, if that's okay with you?"

She could find no good excuse to refuse. "I suppose."

"Wonderful. You have a nice day, now, and enjoy your facial."

"You were listening in!"

He smiled at her, and she knew that, behind his sunglasses, his eyes were full of mischief. "I never said *I* wasn't, sweet face."

Frustration, she discovered, was a great energizer, properly diverted. It shot her so full of adrenaline that she completed all her errands early in the afternoon and had time to spare for a facial and a hairdo. She even debated buying a new dress for the dinner party, but thought better of it. No need to tip her hand so soon. She'd rather make her fashion debut as a bride.

Jeremy was seated in the living room when Annabel came down that evening. To her horror, Luke was next to him and deep in conversation, with Marion an enthralled observer on the side. Both men rose to their feet at her entrance.

"Annabel, you look wonderful. I love your hair." Jeremy took both her hands and kissed her briefly on the mouth.

"Thank you."

"Let me get you a drink, Annabel." Luke kept his distance, to her enormous relief. Both men were wearing suits, but Luke in pearl gray left Jeremy looking like a pallbearer in his black pin stripe. It was grossly unfair, she thought, that a man of forty who hadn't known what it was to own matching pants and jacket eleven years ago, should be such an elegant clothes horse now. Small wonder he found her dowdy.

"Let Jeremy," she replied sweetly. "He knows what I like."

If she'd hoped to disconcert him, she failed. Jeremy abandoned her to apply his talents as a bartender, and Luke moved in without a moment's hesitation. "What did you do to your hair?" he murmered, his finger tracing a circle around her wrist, as though to warn her not to try to escape him. "Get it cut?"

He couldn't have stated more plainly that he didn't like it. "No," she informed him venomously. "I washed it and it shrank."

"Pity you didn't do the same with your tongue," he shot back. "I see you're out of mourning and into military this evening. I've got to say, Annabel, I much prefer you in tattered pink." He cast a disparaging eye at her beige linen tunic dress.

"Wide shoulders and lapels are very much in fashion, for your information."

"Not on you, sweet thing. They make you look like a baked potato on parade."

Annabel thought she'd have a stroke. No one ever spoke to her like this. Only the knowledge of what she'd accomplished that day allowed her to retain her composure. "I suppose I should be insulted by your appalling manners, but nothing you say or do amazes me anymore."

"Well, it amazes me." His finger and thumb joined around her wrist, manacling her to him. "What is it about you, darling Annabel, that makes me say these things, when all I really want is to be alone with you, and pick up where we left off two nights ago? You do know that's what I want, don't you—and, if you dared to be honest, that you want it, too?"

She found herself trapped in his gaze, more helpless to tear her eyes free than her arm. He was right, she feared. It wasn't what he said that mattered, it was the message in his eyes, his touch, that counted. And she knew, too, that her own words were nothing more than shields behind which she made pitiful attempts to protect herself from the impact of his effect on her. "Please," she begged him, "don't say these things to me. We can't play 'what if?' at this late date. Insult me all you like, if it amuses you, but . . ." She drew in a faltering breath, ". . . don't be nice to me. You're wasting your time."

He adjusted his hold on her so that his fingertips were pressed to her pulse. If her words hadn't given her away, the racing of her heart did, and there was no use her denying it. "You're an intractable woman, my Annabel," he said quietly. "How lucky for both of us that I don't give up easily, otherwise I might take you at your word."

Jeremy's parents arrived at that moment, and spared her from damning herself further. Barbara Carson was a vision in smoky amethyst with snakeskin accessories. Annabel saw Luke's brow lift in appreciation. "Now there," he whispered, "is a woman who knows how to dress, and doesn't mind letting the rest of the world know it."

Jeremy reappeared and handed Annabel a glass of sherry. Unreasonably, she wished, just once, that he'd be a little less conservative—or a little more intuitive. If ever there was a time that she could use a stiff drink, it was now. "Luke and I were talking about you when you came in," he began. "He was telling me how much you've changed since you were nineteen."

"That's right," Luke said, with a smile so evil it would have done credit to a barracuda.

Annabel froze. "You mustn't believe everything he says," she protested, casting a nervous eye around to see if anyone else had overheard. Marion was hovering near—wasn't she always?—but Barbara Carson was sipping champagne and chatting with Jake Lewis, Sybil's friend and lawyer, and Annabel's godfather. "He exaggerates, to put it kindly."

"Canapés," Sybil trilled, appearing in the doorway with a tray. Pandora followed behind carrying napkins. "Do sit down, everyone. It makes nibbling so much easier."

Annabel almost tripped Luke in her effort to put as much distance as possible between him and Jeremy. "Why don't you go polish your charm on someone else?" she suggested, elbowing him aside and plunking herself down on the couch. "I wish to sit with my fiancé."

"Don't get yourself all exercised, love," he returned, with a sly wink. "I haven't said anything incriminating—yet."

"You and Luke knew each other well at one time," Aunt Marion began, once dinner was under way, and the edge taken off her appetite, "but you haven't seen each other in years?"

"We lost touch, the way people often do," Annabel rushed to explain. "May I help you to more lamb?"

"I won't refuse." Marion thrust forward her plate, but not even the prospect of food could divert her from the topic Annabel most wished to avoid. "Exactly how are you related, my dear?"

"I . . . um . . . well . . ."

"Cousins?"

"No. Not cousins, exactly."

Three pairs of eyes affixed themselves unwaveringly on Annabel. Her mother and Luke looked expectant; Pandora sat there as if butter wouldn't melt in her mouth. Annabel stared back at them beseechingly. *Help me.*

"You mean there's no actual blood connection?" Marion pursued the subject untiringly between bites.

Jeremy, to Annabel's discomfort, was following the conversation closely, his eyes resting with unwarranted sympathy, she thought, on her face. "We aren't close," she hedged, doing her best to extricate herself.

Relenting, Luke intervened. "Oh, I wouldn't go quite that far," he remarked, then added ambiguously: "but it is a very loose relationship."

"Well," Marion announced, chasing a morsel of mint jelly around her plate, "loose or not, there's a very strong family resemblance. Pandora has a look of you about her."

Annabel choked on a pea.

"If you'd ever met my late husband," Sybil said, attempting to defuse the situation without actually telling a lie, "you'd understand the real meaning of family resemblance. Why, when I look at Pandora's

110

baby pictures, I'm reminded very clearly of how he looked when I first married him. Young," she added defiantly, staring Annabel down.

Annabel's godfather sniggered. Sybil always had that effect on him, and had been known to reduce him to helpless guffaws on occasion. Annabel prayed he'd manage to control himself tonight. Things were quite complicated enough, without his getting carried away.

"I was a very cute baby," Pandora informed the table at large, no doubt feeling she had to do her bit to cover any awkwardness. Annabel knew that Luke had convinced his daughter not to reveal their connection, though she didn't know why. Whatever the reason, she offered silent gratitude that he had.

"And you've grown into a very lovely young lady," Luke told her. "Sybil, this lamb is delicious. My compliments to the chef."

Annabel could have kissed him. All this talk of babies was dangerous and could only lead to more difficult questions. Thank goodness he'd had the brains to see that. She had to admit that, when he put his mind to it, he could charm apples off trees. In no time at all, he had everyone at the table exchanging anecdotes on their favorite foods and restaurants, a topic that even Marion found engrossing.

And it was then that Annabel made a fatal mistake. She relaxed, and even dared to enjoy herself. She laughed at the jokes; she allowed Jake to pour her more wine, twice. She felt her tension draining away and incautiously permitted herself to contemplate Luke's surprisingly fine points.

It afforded her the utmost pleasure to sit back and enjoy him: his turn of phrase, his social ease. She loved the way he treated her mother. She even went so far as to admit to herself that perhaps it had been a mistake to keep him from Pandora. The man sitting at her mother's table tonight had a depth and kindness to him that she wasn't sure she'd appreciated when she'd been nineteen.

Why was it, she wondered, letting her gaze linger on his face, that men aged so much more gracefully than women? At forty, he was even more handsome than he'd been at twenty-nine. Maybe it had something to do with success. To whatever extent he had achieved it, it lent him an assurance that he wore without pretension. She thought he was the most attractive man she'd ever known, and right on the heels of that shocking thought came another: had she drunk too much wine?

Then she caught Jeremy observing her as acutely as she'd been examining Luke, and he looked as if he, too, thought she was a little drunk—an unheard-of occurrence with Annabel. In any event, he wore a most peculiar expression on his face.

It was after nine thirty when the others rose to take coffee and liqueurs in the living room. Annabel was preparing to join them when Pandora caught at her sleeve.

"Can I stay up another half hour, Mom?"

Annabel hesitated. It was past Pandora's bedtime, but she'd hardly spent any time with her daughter lately. "Well . . ."

"No, Pandora." Luke had come back into the room, taking Annabel by surprise with his words. "That's not a good idea."

"But there's no school tomorrow, and this is a special occasion."

112

"I know, honey, but it isn't a good time."

A look passed between the two of them that Annabel couldn't fathom. It spoke volumes, but not for the life of her could she interpret its meaning. Even more astounding was Pandora's capitulation.

"Okay," she agreed, with none of the sullenness that had marked her exchange with her mother the night before. And then she did something that absolutely floored Annabel, and made her come very close to crying. She kissed her mother, then turned to Luke and kissed him, too. "Good night, Daddy," she said, and went up the stairs without another word.

She's waited ten years to be able to call him that, Annabel thought, the enormity of what she'd done to her child suddenly appearing in a new light. All by myself, I've deprived her of the one thing I most missed saying, after my father died. May God forgive me.

"Feel good about what you're doing?" Luke asked Annabel, closing the door behind Pandora so that they were alone in the dining room where no one would overhear them. There was nothing genial about his look or his tone.

She felt suddenly chilled, and very nervous, all her after-dinner glow melting. His disdain was a sobering experience. "I'm not sure I know what you mean," she hedged, wishing she didn't sound so patently insincere.

He sighed as though the whole situation had become too wearying to be endured. "Do you really not see where all your silly lies are leading you, Annie?"

She hated being called a liar, and silly. She hated being called Annie. Come to think of it, she hated him. "They weren't necessary till you showed up."

113

"They're not necessary now, and never were. You have this misguided notion that, by keeping everyone else in the dark, you're in perfect control of your life, when in fact, you're a prisoner of your own warped ideas of acceptability. You're so enmeshed in deception, you can't recognize the truth when it's staring you in the face."

He'd grown quietly furious as he spoke, his anger all the more blistering for its reined intensity. When he made a move toward her, she backed away, and for the first time in years, she actually tasted fear.

Beset by his attack, she tried to play for time. "What truth?"

"You decide not to tell me I have a daughter. You decide not to tell Jeremy who I am. I suppose," he said, pinning her against the buffet, "it really is too much to expect you to tell him that you're prepared to marry him for appearances' sake, even though you're half in love with me?"

"I'm not in love with you." She tried to outstare him, but behind him, the crystal chandelier shimmered brilliantly. It brought tears to her eyes that she told herself had nothing to do with grief or regret. She tried very hard to drum up scorn, and knew only despair.

"Oh, Annie," he said, and his voice rumbled against her mouth like distant thunder, "did you perhaps think no one saw the way you were looking at me across the dinner table? I noticed, Annie, and so did he."

"How did I look at you?" she stammered. "I don't know what you're talking about."

"As if you'd like to be kissed, darling. Would you?" He taunted her mouth with his lips, withholding them just enough to leave her aching with deprivation. "Would you?"

The way he was leaning against her was disgracefully familiar. She could feel every lovely contour, every last masculine configuration. It wasn't her heart that was vibrating the lapels of her tunic dress, but his; not her hands that urged suggestively until there was such an intimate uniting of hip and thigh that she couldn't tell whose blood it was, flickering like fire between them. But they were her eyes that drifted shut with desire, and her arms that stole around his neck. And her tongue that convicted her.

"Yes," she breathed. "Oh, yes! Yes!"

He dropped her like the proverbial hot coal. "Sorry, sweet face, you've got the wrong guy."

"No, I haven't." Blindly, she reached out and hung on to him, afraid she'd fall without his support, afraid she'd lose him forever if she let the moment slip away. And terribly afraid of what her admission meant because, at that moment, she faced the most difficult truth of all.

She might have control of her mind, she discovered, but only then, amid the abandoned remains of the dinner, did she fully understand the refined torture of neglected desire. And with that comprehension came the added recognition that she had little control over her body, and absolutely none over her heart. "All right," she whispered, beaten at last. "You win. I'll talk to Jeremy."

Even as she made the promise, she found herself looking for loopholes. "But not tonight."

"When?"

"Soon."

"You don't have time for 'soon,' Annabel. The wedding's next weekend."

She burst into tears. "Everyone's ganging up on me," she wailed.

Luke wrapped his arms around her and held her close again. "No, my darling, that's not so. You've made some foolish mistakes, and we don't want to see you compound them with another. Call off the wedding, please."

"How come you're all so smart?" She sniffed, tugging his shirt free of his belt and wiping her nose and eyes on it. "Especially you? You hardly know me."

"I know enough to make me think it might be worth spending what's left of my life learning all the rest."

"But all those wedding presents to be returned—all that food. All the gossip!"

"What you have to decide is if they're more important than the people who'll be hurt if this marriage takes place." He shook her lovingly. "Annie, Jeremy deserves better, I deserve better, but most of all, you deserve better."

"Jeremy will be hurt anyway, if I leave him."

Luke privately wondered how true this was. "Better one casualty than three."

"I'll have to find the right way to tell him. Promise you won't try to rush me."

"You've got seven days, Annabel, that's all, and a lot of skeletons to bring out of the closet by then."

"But you'll be there for me, won't you?"

She raised her huge inky-blue eyes and looked forlornly at him, and he had to stop himself from promising he'd take the whole weight of her deception off her shoulders. She was the most infuriating woman in the world, and he feared he loved her to distraction, but it

116

was much too soon to tell her that. He wasn't willing to step in where Jeremy would be leaving off. He wanted to be a lot more than a convenience, or a crutch. It was time for Annabel to grow up, and take responsibility for her life.

"This mess is of your own making, and you're the only one who can undo it," he told her. "When you have, it will be soon enough for us to consider if we have a future."

It was the biggest gamble he'd ever undertaken, and the thought that it might not pay off almost made him ill. But he had to know she would come to him without reservation; that she'd sacrifice all her false gods, just to be with him.

She looked shattered at his words. "You mean, you'll let me ruin all my wedding plans on the off-chance that you might want me afterward? My God, why would I do that, when you already left me once to fend for myself?"

"Because if the love's real, there's trust, and you don't need guarantees."

"I *want* guarantees," she wailed anew. "I played with fire before with you, and I won't get burnt a second time."

"Then I'll give you one," he promised coldly. "You go ahead with your appalling deceit, and I guarantee you'll wither like a rosebud caught in an early frost. You'll use up all your youth and sweetness racing into old age, because you think that's safe, and you won't be hurt by anything. You'll refuse to think about the man you married, in case you find he hates you for trapping him in a loveless marriage. And it will be loveless, Annabel. It's obvious there's no passion, no desire, in your feelings for Jeremy."

"What if I've decided I don't need them?"

God help him if, for once, she was telling the truth. "Then I'd say that, in your case, brains were a liability," he replied, deceptively soft-spoken. "You may be able to program your thoughts when you're awake, but what do you dream of when you lie in bed in your long, romantic nightgowns, with the satin kissing your skin like a lover?"

How did she admit that, until he came back into her life, she hadn't let herself dream? That she'd been satisfied to be spared the nightmares that came from caring too deeply? And how could she seriously contemplate destroying the security she'd found with Jeremy, for the tenuous joy of loving Luke?

He might be able to touch her heart the way no other man could, but his insensitivity to her needs and concerns terrified her. She'd disintegrate if she had to go through another loss such as she'd suffered with him before.

There might not be any dynamics in her relationship with Jeremy, but neither were there any threats. She would survive with him. Maybe, she concluded, a woman was not meant to marry the great love of her life. Marriage was too frail a thing to be exposed to the energy of such a force.

"Well, Annabel?"

She pushed away from him. "I don't dream," she told him stonily.

Liar, liar, her little voice chanted.

Perhaps, she flung back as she left the room, but he doesn't have to know that.

Oh Christ, Luke thought, sliding into the nearest chair. What am I going to do now?

What if he'd pushed too hard? What if the look he

118

thought he saw in her eyes wasn't love, and he was seeing only what he wanted to see? What if he'd blown everything by refusing to act as her safety net?

Out in the front hall, he heard voices, and the sound of the front door opening and closing. The guests had departed, no doubt all atwitter that two members of the dinner party had chosen not to join them for coffee.

"Well," he muttered, making his way by the connecting door into the living room, "it's not too late for the liqueurs, even if the coffee is cold. I feel like getting very drunk."

"Then start pouring," Jeremy said from the depths of a wing chair. "And I'll join you."

CHAPTER EIGHT

Annabel went upstairs, intending to look in on Pandora, then go to her own room, put Luke's accusations firmly out of her mind, and get enough rest to be able to face tomorrow like the independent adult she was supposed to be, instead of some mindless wimp whose hormones were out of whack. Instead, she locked herself in her bathroom and bawled her eyes out.

Vladimir Pryzjolenska, seeing the way of things to come, had fled Russia in the 1920s with nothing in his pocket but the curved needles with which he sewed together his priceless furs. He'd settled in Canada, changed his name to Pryce, and plied his trade to feed himself and his wife and son.

About the same time, Liam Fitzgerald had thumbed his nose at a family hidebound by tradition, and come to North America with no assets beyond a beguiling voice and a pair of hands that could gentle the most spirited horse—or woman.

Each had been possessed of a courage and energy beside which their eventual fortunes had paled. Annabel wondered, mopping up a fresh outpouring of tears, how a fearful, indecisive creature such as herself could possibly be their granddaughter.

She was thirty years old, she didn't know who she

wanted or how she felt. She wasn't sure if she loved Jeremy, or Luke, or either of them. At that moment, all she knew was that she felt like a lost child, and she wanted her mother.

Sybil opened her bedroom door at Annabel's knock, took one look at her daughter's face, and drew her inside. "Drink this," she commanded bracingly, and poured Annabel a stiff brandy from the decanter by the bed.

"Don't tell me you've become a closet alcoholic, Mother," Annabel muttered resentfully. She wanted to be cuddled, not pickled. "It's the last thing I need to hear today."

"It's medicinal," Sybil maintained, trying very hard to look wan.

Annabel had forgotten, in her inventory of familial talents, to add "dramatic." Her mother had missed her true calling. "To cure what ills—or do I want to know?"

"Well, darling child, after that fiasco of a dinner party, I needed something fortifying to get me through the night. As if it's not enough to have to listen to Marion ferreting out the fine print of your life, I have to endure her ravenous attacks on anything remotely edible. I tell you, I'm almost afraid to sit too still, in case she takes a bite out of me!"

Annabel collapsed in an easy chair next to the window, and kicked off her shoes. "You deserve her, for dumping Luke on me. Mother, I don't think I can take another week of his nagging."

"Nagging?" Sybil looked as affronted as if someone had accused her of harboring a psychopath in her house. "Luke *nagging*? Why, Annabel, I can't imagine what you mean. He's the most amenable creature in the world."

"He's doing his best to create total havoc of my life."

Sybil's efforts to appear disturbed were thwarted by the pleased smile that insisted on creeping over her face. "Now how could he possibly do that, if you're as sure as you claim to be that you're doing exactly what you want to do?"

"Mother!" Consigning moderation to hell, Annabel choked down a healthy swig of brandy. It did revive her somewhat. "I came here looking for a little maternal support, not to hear you defend the man who's already caused me more unhappiness than any other single human being."

"But he didn't realize he was doing that."

"That doesn't give him the right to come back and do it a second time."

"Don't wave your arms like that, child, that's Waterford crystal." Sybil reached out and rescued her snifter. "Just explain to me how he's managing to cause you so much upset."

"With your help, I suspect, but the worst of it is, he's beginning to undermine *my* confidence in my own values."

"How is he doing that?"

"He wants me to cancel the wedding, for a start, on the strength of his belief that I'm more in love with him than Jeremy."

"Are you, darling?"

It was a question she was no longer prepared to consider. "Honestly, Mother, do I sound like a woman in love? I could strangle him without a moment's remorse."

122

"I understand just what you're saying. I felt the same way about your father, at least once a week. And I adored him, as you know." Sybil perched on the side of the bed, striving not to look complacent. "What else, dear?"

Annabel practically snorted with indignation. "He thinks Jeremy should know who Pandora's father is, and never mind if it revives old scandal and casts a pall on the most important day of my life."

"I think he's right."

"He calls me a liar, Mother." Annabel ignored the interruption, intent only on strengthening her case against him.

Sybil examined her manicure. "I'm sure he doesn't really mean that. He's probably angry with you for deceiving him about Pandora. After all, you did rob him of ten years of her life."

The two of them were in cahoots! She should have known better than to expect her mother to side with her. "Well there's not much I can do about that, now."

"That's not entirely true, you know. You could come out and tell everyone that he's her father, so that he can enjoy her company without having to worry about revealing what is, after all, your . . ." Sybil paused, delicately. ". . . er . . . your self-imposed reticence. I mean, give credit where it's due, darling. He's certainly not ashamed of his part in all this, nor has he made any att npt to wriggle out of his responsibilities since he got here. It seems to me the least you can do now is to acknowledge him publicly, and let him know that he's welcome to visit her again, and have her visit him."

"Give him permission to keep on interfering in my

123

life?" Annabel was thunderstruck. "I'd be out of my mind to do anything of the sort."

"You might just as well be gracious about it, Annabel, because there's not much you can do to prevent it. I'm sure Pandora won't give him up, not after finding him after all these years."

There was a moment's silence, then Sybil went on, warming up to her subject in a way that made Annabel highly suspicious of her motives: "You know what would be a really nice gesture, my lamb?"

"No, but I'm sure you're going to tell me, Mother."

"Don't sound so alarmed, dear. It's nothing arduous or injurious to your health, but it wouldn't hurt you to give him a couple of hours of your time and go through all those albums we have stored in the attic. They're full of pictures of Pandora from the day she was born—all her birthday parties, and the time she was a mushroom in the school musical, and all that sort of thing. It's not quite the same as being there, but it would give him some idea of what she was like as she grew up."

She poured herself a snifter of brandy. "And if that doesn't work," Sybil murmured, twirling the glass gently, "it won't be for lack of trying."

Annabel's guard went up. "Trying what, Mother?"

"To be fair," Sybil returned with faultless logic. "Did you say good night to Jeremy?"

"I was going to, but I'd come upstairs to check on Pandora, and the next thing, everyone was leaving, so I thought I'd call him in the morning." Another lie, but what was one more at this stage? And she was ashamed of her emotional outburst. What had it accomplished, after all?

"But darling, he didn't leave with all the others.

124

He's waiting downstairs to see you. He was quite concerned when you didn't join us after dinner."

Annabel felt the bottom fall out of her stomach. "Oh, Mother!" she gasped, leaping out of the chair. "Why in the world didn't you tell me that earlier?"

"Well, it's only been about half an hour," Sybil protested.

Half an hour? "Where's Luke?"

"Keeping him company, I shouldn't doubt. Does it matter?"

Matter? Oh, thought Annabel wrathfully, if her mother wasn't a bare-faced schemer, she was almost certainly senile.

Things were much worse downstairs than she'd envisioned. The two men were sitting across from each other, an almost empty bottle of Benedictine on the table between them. They looked up at her appearance and exchanged telling glances. They'd discarded their jackets and loosened their ties. They had about them such an air of masculine comradeship that Annabel's blood froze. Unfortunately, her tongue wagged twice as hard to make up for it.

"Whatever he's been telling you," she informed Jeremy rashly, "is a pack of lies, except for the part about who Pandora's father is, and it's him—he. A long time ago. Before I met you. Before Pandora was born."

"That makes biological sense," Jeremy replied, and sniggered at Luke, whose immoderate laughter caused him to slide out of his chair and onto the carpet.

"You're both drunk!" Outraged, she glared at them. Here she was, *agonizing* over the past, the future, and

125

all the bits and pieces in between, and the pair of them were practically incoherent.

"Plastered," Luke slurred, crawling back into his chair with the coordination of a backward two-year-old. "Would you care to join us?"

"I would like you to disappear," she informed him with icy dignity, "preferably off the face of the earth, but failing that, anywhere else you please. I would like to be alone with my fiancé."

"Okay, but be kind to him, he's a very nice guy, and he's my friend."

Annabel had to restrain herself from kicking him. Since when had a fox been anyone's friend? "Oh, Jeremy," she began, as soon as they were alone, "I'm sure he's told you all kinds of things, but—"

"Nothing I didn't already know."

Annabel's mouth felt as dry as sand. "What do you mean?"

Jeremy placed his glass on the table and took her hands in his. "Dear Annabel," he said, with such infinite compassion that she felt her eyes swimming again, "I have known since the day Luke arrived here that he is Pandora's father."

"Who told you?"

He smiled at her, and shook his head. She realized then that he was not nearly as drunk as she'd first thought. He was merely less cautious than usual. "No one, my love. No one had to, she is so clearly his child. Not even your agitation was needed to alert me to the fact of his identity. I cannot imagine anyone missing the connection."

She was appalled. "You mean, your parents guessed —and your aunt? Oh, Jeremy, how embarrassing for you. Are you terribly upset?"

"Not for the reasons you suppose. I think I'm shocked . . ."

Annabel pulled her hands free and covered her face, wondering how much worse things were going to get before they improved. "You must have known—"

"That she had a father? Of course, and I expected that, eventually, you'd feel able to tell me about him. What I hadn't realized, until a few days ago, is that you see me as such an ogre that you would put yourself through this sort of hell rather than confide in me, and that's what upsets me, Annabel."

She felt terribly ashamed, and could offer no answer that would mitigate her lack of faith in him.

He reached over and removed her hands from her face. "Why are you afraid of him, my love?"

"Afraid?" What else had he noticed, with his fine eye for detail? "I'm not afraid of him."

Jeremy looked at her, long and searchingly. "Then why are you afraid of yourself?"

She promptly burst into tears again, and tried to hide from him. He'd never seen her cry before, and she didn't want him to see her now, with her face all distorted and ugly. Her pride was all she had left. "He's a horrible man, and I hate him for coming between us with his insinuations."

Jeremy pulled her against him, and stroked her back, the way she'd wanted her mother to, upstairs. "He's a very fine man—a very strong man, I believe, and capable of great love. It would be a pity, I think, for you to deny that."

He made her feel small and ungenerous with his observations. "Yes," she sighed, leaning into his shoulder and drawing on his strength. "It's perhaps a good thing that Pandora has met him."

He put her from him quite forcefully. "Don't over-simplify what I'm saying, Annabel. He'll be good for Pandora, but only if you'll allow him to be."

"Oh, I will, I will." There was a warning in his voice that frightened her. She felt like a castaway, stranded in some remote place with no one to help her. "I talked to my mother, and I see that I've handled the situation badly. I'll talk to him, in the morning, and we'll come to an understanding about things."

Jeremy looked as if he would like to say more; as if, she thought, he wanted to explain that she still hadn't understood what he was trying to tell her. But at the last moment, he changed his mind. "In that case," he said, rising and picking up his jacket, "I probably won't see you till Monday. My mother tells me she's hosting a bridal tea in your honor tomorrow after-noon, to which the men are not invited, and I'm on call tomorrow night. Spend what time you have to spare sorting things out with him."

He kissed her as if he were saying good-bye forever, instead of for two days, and she clung to him again, anxiety a vague ache inside her that she couldn't dispel. "Do you have to leave?"

He nodded. "I must. Walk me to the door?"

Depressed, she watched him drive off. Paradoxically, she'd never loved him so much, nor been more aware that she didn't love him enough.

The weather had changed, and a soft, persistent rain had rolled in across the coast from the Pacific. At this time of year, it could turn out to be a passing overnight disturbance, or one that lasted the rest of the month. A week ago, she'd have worried that it might spoil her wedding day. Now, it didn't matter at all. The day was ruined anyway.

* * *

She timed things very carefully the next afternoon, leaving just one hour after lunch for her meeting with Luke in the attic. "I'll show you where all the albums are, and you can spread yourself out on the old desk up there and browse all afternoon, if you like," she told him. She wasn't about to let him think she wanted to spend more time than necessary alone with him.

The house had been built in the days when materials were plentiful and labor cheap. At one end of the upper hall, a door opened onto a second staircase which, in turn, led up to yet another heavy door that gave entrance to the dormered attic. It had been Annabel's favorite retreat when she was an adolescent. In winter, she'd curl up on the old velvet fainting couch that had once graced her grandmother's bedroom, and read tragic romances. She always took on the heroine's character, and had wept bitterly when, as Anna Karenina or some other ill-fated lady, she'd lost her true love.

Her mother had thought her preoccupation with unhappy endings was most unhealthy, and she'd come up with a thermos of hot chocolate and drag Annabel out of her latest reverie. They'd sit on the padded window seat, and look out across the windy Strait of Georgia, and Sybil would tell her about the great love of her life: Annabel's father.

The winter before she went to Hawaii was the last that Annabel had spent up there. Her own tragedy, the following spring, had catapulted her out of adolescence and into womanhood too cruelly for her to find solace in childish pursuits anymore, and the attic had reverted to its former role as storage for things seldom used, or outgrown.

129

It smelled musty, and was full of secret shadows that afternoon. The rain hadn't blown inland, and summer mist hugged the coast. Annabel made her way through the collection of trunks and discarded furniture, and switched on a brass gooseneck lamp that sat on the big pedestal desk in one of the dormers.

"What a fantastic room!" Luke was enthralled, pushing aside anything that got in his way as he went from one window to another, and peered out. "Annabel, look at the view from up here. On a clear day—"

"I know," she finished for him, opening the desk drawers and hauling out the albums, "You can see forever."

"We've got to come up here again, when the mist clears."

Not on your life, Annabel thought. "Well, now you know where the place is, feel free." She intended to do what she'd promised Jeremy and her mother she'd do, as concisely and impersonally as possible, and no more. Luke could rummage around all he liked, but she wouldn't keep him company.

She'd done a lot of thinking last night, got herself firmly back on track, and come to some rational conclusions. She would accept Luke's right to a share in Pandora's life, but her own was none of his business. To jeopardize all her plans because she fancied herself in danger of falling in love with him was unrealistic and immature. She should have outgrown that sort of stuff when she stopped assuming the role of distressed heroine during her teens.

She stacked the albums at one end of the desk. "We may as well get started. I'm going out later, and I still have to change."

He didn't answer, didn't make a move to join her.

130

"Did you hear what I said?" Impatiently, she turned around, and found herself alone. "Luke?"

"Aaargh!" He leapt out from behind a huge old wardrobe, a dustsheet over his head, his arms flailing wildly.

She didn't know how she contained her shriek. "Don't be such a damn fool, Luke. I don't have all day."

"Sometimes, Annie," he complained, tossing the sheet aside and running his fingers through his hair, "you're no fun at all."

Good, she thought. Fun, like happiness, usually proved costly. "I've arranged these in order." She sniffed, hoping to convey her utter disdain with his antics. "This pink silk one is her baby book, and it records everything she did for the first year—her first smile and tooth, a lock of hair, a footprint, the works— as well as dozens of photographs. The others cover the years after that."

He joined her at the desk, standing altogether too close. "I really appreciate this, Annabel. Can we sit on the couch to look through them?"

"Sit anywhere you please," she replied offhandedly. "Now that I've explained things to you, I'm going down to get dressed for the bridal tea my future mother-in-law is giving for me this afternoon."

He looked crestfallen. "You mean you're leaving me already?"

Yes, she thought, that's exactly what I'm doing, and the pity of it is that I didn't leave you years ago, instead of hoarding the secret memory of you. "I'm leaving."

He gazed at her. "Okay, Annie."

"So?"

He continued to focus those wonderful gray eyes on

her face. She could feel them caressing her, along with the lazy warmth in his voice. "So what?" He was almost smiling.

"So get out of my way. I can't walk through you."

He released a little bit more of his smile, just enough to touch his eyes with silver. "Of course not. How stupid of me."

He made a fractional concession to her request. She could get by, with a little body contact. Or she could insist he allow her more space, and in doing so, admit she was afraid to touch him. Holding in her breath—and her breasts—she sidled past him, averting her face.

He sidled with her. "Why won't you look at me, darling Annabel?"

That voice of his should be outlawed. It stole inside her clothing and kissed her in places that made her blush. She wished she had the wit to come up with a snappy answer, but it was all she could do to remain upright.

His arm swung up beside her neck, so that the only way to get past him was to duck down and wriggle across his chest and hips. The mere thought of what that would entail stopped her in her tracks. She stared steadfastly at the door, twenty-five impossible feet away.

He expelled a sigh that teased her ear with pleasure. "I rinsed," he whispered, "and all my hung-over baboon breath is supposed to have been purified."

She choked on a giggle that took her completely by surprise, and clapped a hand to her mouth.

Alarmingly, he removed it with his, and settled his lips on her palm for long, quiet seconds. A tempest began to build in Annabel—a wild, frightening thing.

132

She tugged at her hand, but he held it more securely and impudently allowed his tongue to explore the hollow of her palm: a slight, invisible movement, as shattering in its effect as the tsunami that had first driven her into his arms eleven years ago, in Maui.

She let out an anguished cry and wrenched herself free. Nearly blind with fear, she rushed to the door, scraping her shins on the obstacles between her and escape. The feel of the doorknob beneath her fingers could not have spelled more merciful deliverance had she been fleeing from the devil himself. So great was her relief, it took her several seconds to realize the door itself was not responding to her efforts to open it. Flinging her entire weight at it, she fought to turn the knob, her agitation multiplying along with her heartbeat. It wouldn't budge.

"It appears to be stuck," he said at her shoulder. "Perhaps I can help."

"Get away from me!" Frantically, she renewed her efforts to be free of him, for once and for all, but not all her rattling or banging made the slightest impression. The door was a solid plank of oak, at least two inches thick, with hinges built to withstand anything she could offer in the way of punishment. She was heaving with exertion, her hands bruised and sore, by the time she accepted defeat.

"If you think . . . you've accomplished anything . . . by this," she panted at last, ". . . you're sadly mistaken. I'll simply shout for help . . . until . . . someone hears me." If she could ever draw sufficient air into her beleaguered lungs.

"Don't hold your breath, Annabel," he advised her with finely engineered irony. He was lolling negligently against the window frame of the dormer that

133

looked down on the front of the house, completely unperturbed and thoroughly enjoying the situation. "Your mother just drove off with Pandora and Marion. I guess they're on their way to the bridal tea which it looks as if you're going to miss."

She flew across the room and pressed her nose to the glass, just in time to see her mother's silver Jaguar pulling out of the driveway. Even as she watched, its elegant length slid out of sight. She could have howled with frustration and rage.

Instead, she turned on Luke and made him the recipient of her invective. "You snake!" she hissed. "You despicable, deceiving oaf! This is all your doing and don't think I don't know it. I hope . . . I hope . . ." Oh, she had insults to spare for him, and she'd let him hear them. She would. Once she'd swallowed the lump of outrage in her throat. ". . . I hope I live to see the day you're as miserable as you've made me."

Then, like the sophisticated, controlled adult she prided herself on being, she buried her face in her hands and sobbed noisily. It was too much. He was too much.

"Ann—abel!" His voice flowed over her like dark velvet, smoothing all her ruffled agitation, as his arms came around her and turned her to him. Wrapping her in comfort and protection, he ran his hands up and down her back, soothing and quieting her.

She made a heroic effort to hang on to her justified rage. She really did. But it proved as elusive as the mist outside the windows, and no more capable of withstanding the sunshine, for Luke's concern was as warm and tangible as anything a summer day could produce. Slowly, all the fear and anger filtered away, until only the exhausted hiccups of her sobs remained to punctuate the silence with reminders of her outburst.

Closing her eyes, she slumped against his chest and conceded defeat. It was one thing to lie alone in her bed and theorize on how she should conduct herself, and another matter entirely to resist the messages of his heart and hers, thundering together in quiet harmony. What was the use of pretending she was made of marble, when every part of her was dissolving with hunger?

She didn't know when her distress inched into desire, or when her hands uncurled from their clenched fury to slide down the narrowing band of his waist. She only knew that when he kissed her this time, he released in her a yearning that would not allow her to clutter the magic with irrelevancies. She melted under that kiss, her resistance toppling. The way her mouth softened and her body bent to his was a tacit admission that all her former objections had been lies, just as he'd always maintained they were.

There was nothing, and no one, except this moment, this place, and the two of them. And now she saw that all the years between this time and the very first time he'd kissed her had been a penance to be endured until they could come together again.

When he swung her up in his arms, she clung to him with her lips and hands, and bound him to her forever. She opened her eyes and he saw that they were flowing over with the love and passion she'd tried so hard to deny only the night before.

He carried her across the dim and dusty attic, stepping over and around things that would impede him, until he found a place where he could love her again. And neither of them said a word. What need was there, when their eyes and mouths were in such perfect communion, and their bodies alive with passion?

If he had been a memorable lover before, he was unforgettable now. The undressing of her was a ceremony so full of reverence that it left no room for false modesty; a rite so sacred that it could not be rushed. And the sight of her, naked at last before him, a vision to be adored.

Annabel, quivering with need, felt her heart flying around behind her ribs like a thing gone mad. Control —what was that? What did it mean? What did it matter?

His hands defined her, full of wonder for the fragility and softness of her as he fondled her breasts, her buttocks, her thighs and every inch of her. He was filled with the scent of her, a summer bouquet of exquisite delicacy. His eyes, slate dark with desire, devoured her, following his hands as he explored and loved her body which had been aching for his touch all these years. His lovemaking was firing her to such passionate response that she felt as threatened as if he were holding her at the brink of sanity.

But when his mouth discovered her, traveling to her core to taste the full wonder of her, she tilted over the edge, a plea escaping her that he not let her go alone, and at the sound, he released her just long enough to tear off his own clothing.

She looked at him, dazzled by the carved beauty of him, and uncaring that her gaze possessed him as only a lover's can. He entered her at once, the strength and vigor of him miraculously fitting perfectly with her slender elegance. He absorbed her and overpowered her, thrusting and flowing until sensibility was no more than a prick of light in the darkness of the universe, and he and she were forged together in the fire of their loving.

He loved her thoroughly, taking her higher and higher, carrying her on a melody of sighs, a symphony of passion, that escalated to such a finale that she could not bear it a moment longer, and shattered into a thousand spangled prisms of ecstasy with him.

The rain dripped noiselessly from the eaves, and the sea mist crept up to the windows concealingly, so that no one but the gods knew that Luke and Annabel had found each other again. And the gods were smiling, because there, on her grandmother's old velvet fainting couch, Luke reclaimed what he'd so carelessly cast aside eleven years earlier; and in doing so, he taught her that nothing she had dreamed about when she was a young girl could hold a candle to the splendor of this long-awaited reality.

And after, they stayed there, naked bodies entwined while their separate thoughts tried to come to grips with what had happened. He contemplated the fullness in his heart and recognized it for what it was. And he was full of amazement and gratitude to find himself forty years old and at last understanding the depth and dimensions of love. Until he found her again, it had always seemed a fine and inconceivable madness that afflicted other men, not him.

He touched her beautiful body again, to be certain he was not dreaming. Annabel turned her face into his neck in disbelief. The loneliness and the mystery of love she'd known and grieved over for years, but the poetry of it—that was not something she'd ever taken into account. She felt it now. In Luke's arms, she'd been thoroughly loved . . . and touched by the poetry.

CHAPTER NINE

Time lost all dimension, and they might have stayed there the rest of the afternoon, if the sound of a car stopping at the front door hadn't scattered the magic, and galvanized Annabel into leaping off the couch and trying to gather up her clothes. How could they have become so scattered and tangled with Luke's?

"Don't stare," she ordered him, ridiculously self-conscious, all things considered, at the way he lounged there, never taking his eyes off her body. "And please get up. They've come home early, probably because I didn't appear at the tea, and this will be the first place they'll look—and oh, dear! Whatever am I going to offer as an excuse?"

Unabashedly aroused by the sight of her prancing around like a wood sprite, Luke was enjoying himself too much to worry about being caught in his birthday suit. "I have nothing to hide, darling Annie."

That wasn't true, Annabel thought. He had plenty to conceal and she couldn't help but notice it. She found herself wondering how he'd manage to get all of him back into his clothes, without taking a cold shower first. Unbidden, a little smile crept across her mouth, and for a moment, she wallowed in the pleasure of their stolen afternoon. The sound of her mother calling her name in the downstairs hall restored her sense of propriety with a distinct shock, and sent her scurrying to locate the rest of her clothes.

Her panties were nowhere to be found. No amount of rummaging around unearthed them. "My underwear is missing," she whispered, horrified.

Luke had managed to stir himself sufficiently to climb into his jeans, and even zip up the fly. "Well, don't look at me," he whispered back, rolling his eyes at her. "I'm not wearing it."

"Annabel, dear heart, are you up there?" Sybil caroled from the foot of the attic stairs.

A terrified squeak escaped Annabel's lips, and she flung him an imploring look. "Help me."

"No need to panic, my darling," he told her calmly, handing her her cotton dress. "Slip into this, and no normal person will think to ask what you're wearing underneath it."

Her hands were shaking so badly, she couldn't do up the buttons, even though they were large as silver dollars. "Help me," she begged again, an edge of hysteria creeping into her voice. It seemed to be an ongoing refrain with her of late.

He had her done up in no time, and was across the room in a flash, dragging her behind him. A quick flick of the wrist, and two of the albums were spread open on the desk, the others in a heap on the floor, and looking for all the world as if they'd been examined from cover to cover.

"Sit," he commanded, and thrust her down on the old swivel chair that sat before the desk. When the door finally opened, he was leaning over her shoulder, apparently absorbed in a picture of Pandora on her ninth birthday.

"There you are!" Sybil exclaimed. "My darlings, we were wondering what on earth could have happened, and we thought the time must just have got away from you, didn't we, Marion?"

Swinging around in the chair, Annabel found herself confronted by her mother, whose expression could not be described as anything other than self-satisfied, and Marion, who looked like an affronted weasel. "Hello, everyone," Annabel said weakly. "The door stuck."

It was the lamest excuse in the world, and she shot Luke an accusing glare, to which he responded with a shrug.

"Yes, we know," Sybil said, and Annabel belatedly realized that her mother had opened the door from the outside, without any assistance at all from Luke on the inside. So, he hadn't been responsible for what had happened, but it didn't take much mental agility to put two and two together and figure out who had. Sybil had never looked more like the Cheshire cat in all her born days.

"I saw the problem, the minute we got up here," Sybil went on blithely. "The lock had jammed from the outside. Hadn't it, Marion?"

Marion clacked her teeth together and fixed her eyes suspiciously on something near the fainting couch. "So it would seem," she sniffed.

Following her gaze, Annabel saw with unspeakable dismay that her underpants were draped over a lampshade, and right in Marion's line of vision. Uncaring that she would simply invoke further suspicion by doing so, she clutched at Luke's thigh, her face ashen, and flung an agonized glance to where the lingerie was spread out and waiting to convict her.

140

"We thought we were going to have to send out flares," Luke boomed, planting himself squarely between the underwear and the aunt. "Marion, you have no idea how relieved I am to see you." With one hand, he hauled her to him and planted a kiss on her cheek, while with the other he swept up the incriminating evidence and stuffed it in his hip pocket.

"What are you trying to hide, young man?" Marion demanded, not about to be diverted.

"Not a thing, dear lady," he replied.

"Well, *something* is hanging out of your pocket."

"His handkerchief," Sybil declared, swooping down and tucking the lace frill that edged her daughter's panties firmly out of view. "Come along, everyone, I think we could all use a drink, and you, my darling . . ." She had the nerve to fix Annabel in a reproving stare. ". . . You must call Mrs. Carson and apologize profusely for missing the tea, which was absolutely delicious."

Annabel didn't know which impressed her more: her mother's shameless manipulation, or her unmitigated gall.

There was scarcely an opportunity to exchange two words with Luke after that. Marion appointed herself Annabel's watchdog, surmising, correctly, that her nephew's best interests were not being served by Luke's presence in the house. She followed Annabel about the place like a second shadow, and the only time Annabel knew any peace and quiet was when she was in her bedroom.

All of which seemed to suit Luke, she thought miserably, avoiding the inquisitive looks her mother kept directing her way. He resumed his role as Sybil's favorite houseguest as though nothing at all untoward had occurred. If it bothered him that they'd betrayed Jeremy, he managed to keep the fact well hidden from Annabel. One thing was certain: Luke hadn't felt impelled to vindicate her honor by offering to marry her instead. He hadn't said he loved her, and now that he'd had his way with her, didn't even seem particularly anxious to look at her, or try to determine how she might be feeling. She half expected he'd be catching the next flight back to Toronto. Wasn't that how the movie ended before?

But, she'd reckoned without Pandora, whose appeal to Luke, apparently, was of more enduring stuff.

"Mom!" Pandora came racing into the living room after dinner on Monday evening, her face pink with excitement, and skidded to a halt before the couch where Annabel sat. "Luke says he'll take me to see the hot-air balloons tomorrow, if it's okay with you. Can I go? Can I?"

"May I," Annabel corrected automatically. Four days, eighteen hours and seven minutes from now, she'd be Mrs. Jeremy Carson, unless she took steps to prevent it. And that seemed a mammoth undertaking, far beyond her capabilities. Since yesterday, her life had taken on the gauzy unreality of a nightmare, and she was too consumed with pain to care about anything so mundane as hot-air balloons, unless one could be commissioned to carry her far away from this scene of impending disaster.

"If the weather clears," Luke interjected, coming to sit at the opposite end of the couch, and lifting Pandora onto his lap. Marion, demolishing after-dinner mints, immediately heaved herself out of her chair and planted her ample hips between them, intent on not missing a word they might exchange.

"The weatherman says it will," Pandora bubbled. "Please, Mommy, can I?"

Annabel felt like screaming. How could they be so consumed with tomorrow's weather that they couldn't see the guilt and misery written all over her face?

Guilt and misery, nothing! her little voice chimed in. *How about possibly pregnant again? Have you thought of that?*

Annabel felt the blood drain out of her face. Another illegitimate child? Another scandal? She'd rather die.

"There's high pressure building off the coast," Luke informed the room at large.

"How lovely," Marion declared pointedly. "Just in time for Saturday. You know what they say, Annabel: happy the bride the sun shines on."

Luke directed a glance over the top of Marion's head, interested to see how Annabel reacted to the comment. Quite frankly, it had his stomach in knots. There were still a few days left, but he had to admit his nerves were wearing thin. Short of a miracle, it didn't seem she'd come to her senses in time. Look at her, sitting there like a porcelain princess, while the precious minutes ticked away like sand through an hourglass. He wanted to shake her.

Across the room, Sybil caught his eye and gave him an encouraging wink, as though to assure him all was not yet lost. Well, he hoped she knew her daughter better than he did, because unless Annabel made some radical decisions pretty fast, he'd have to play his last card and hope it came up trumps. And that was cutting things a bit too close, even for a gambling man.

Christ, Annabel, get it together! he thought, flinging her another glance, and caught her wiping away a surreptitious tear with one finger.

Well, hallelujah, she wasn't made of stone after all! Never mind if she was acting as if nothing had changed; he wouldn't accept that, not after the way she'd come alive in his arms yesterday. And not after catching that sneaky tear trickling down her cheek. Give him half an hour with her, and he'd break her down, or die in the attempt.

Marion, however, was indefatigable in her surveillance. He tried every way he knew how to get Annabel alone someplace where they wouldn't be disturbed, but if the aunt didn't conspire to keep them apart, something else did.

"Come with us to see the hot-air balloons," he invited Annabel and Sybil over breakfast the next morning, certain he could count on Sybil to keep Pandora occupied for an hour or so while he went to work on Annabel. It was Tuesday: three days to countdown.

"We'd love to," Marion chirped, and Luke astonished even himself at the stringent oaths he was tempted to direct at her for her presumption. Damn the woman! She was the Carsons' relative; why couldn't they do their share of keeping her entertained?

"You said we'd go alone," Pandora reminded him, flinging a dismayed glance at Marion, whose declaration that not all children were lovable Pandora had never forgiven. "We have to have our secret conference." She spoke in hushed tones, imparting an urgency to the words.

A spasm of mirth almost overcame Luke at Marion's dilemma, caught as she was between fried ham and eggs, and curiosity. "So we have," he agreed, but resolved to take precautionary measures that day, in case he had to put his emergency plan into operation. Pandora, apprised of the situation, would be a willing accomplice, he was sure.

Annabel wasn't home when they returned that evening. She'd agreed to take a late shift at the hospital, in exchange for someone else taking her classes on Friday, so that she could have the day before the wedding free. Since she was also scheduled to teach first thing the next morning, Sybil explained, she'd arranged to spend that night in one of the nurses' residences, and save herself miles of driving back and forth to the hospital.

More like save herself having to face him, Luke thought, chafing with frustration at yet another delay. It absolutely baffled him how a woman of her intelligence could be such an ostrich. Did she really think, by sticking her head in the sand this way, that she could avoid the catastrophe toward which she was headed? Not if he could help it. Tomorrow was Wednesday; two days to countdown, and no more time to lose.

He made up his mind that he'd get Annabel to himself before another night had passed, if he had to hogtie Marion to do so. But when Annabel came home the next day, she went straight to her room, and didn't even come down for dinner, pleading a headache that she couldn't manage to shake. A pretty fishy excuse, Luke decided, and tried to sneak up to her room while everyone else was finishing dessert. He found her door locked, and before he had a chance to try to persuade her to let him in, the aunt was snapping at his heels like an eager terrier.

"Our little bride needs her rest," Marion announced, "and if there is something she needs, either I or her mother will see that she gets it."

"Er . . . I'm sure you will," he replied, wondering how she'd managed to haul all that weight up the stairs so speedily.

"I intend to leave my bedroom door open throughout the night," she continued ominously, "in case anyone tries to disturb her."

"Very thoughtful of you, I'm sure," he said, and made up his mind on the spot that drastic measures were called for.

Annabel didn't really have a headache. She was locked in her bedroom, in the dark, nursing a heartache that felt mortally wounding, and striving to deal with the problems that were causing it.

The plain fact of the matter was that she loved two men. The one she was scheduled to marry in two and a half days offered her security and contentment. She and Jeremy shared common interests, mutual friends, similar backgrounds—all the things the experts claimed were essential to a successful marriage. On top of that, he was handsome, assured, and above all, good.

And Luke? What could she say about him that was praiseworthy? Not a thing. He was a philanderer, oblivious to the finer points of honor between men. He made fun of the things that were important to her. He was a rogue, altogether too good-looking, and shameless in his sexual expertise. He could transport her with a kiss, took advantage of her at every turn, but wasn't willing to make a lifelong commitment to her. A cavalier, just as she'd always maintained. And she loved him. Given the opportunity, she'd follow him to the ends of the earth.

That's not love, she told herself. That's agony. Love is the comfortable affection you share with Jeremy; something you can live with on a day-to-day basis, without it tearing out your guts. Forget Sunday afternoon and get on with your life. The Carsons think you're the ideal wife for their son. Live up to their expectations.

You're also a liar and a cheat, dearie, her alter ego chipped in, *which no doubt accounts for the fact that Luke's given no indication he's willing to relieve Jeremy of you. He knows what sort of a bargain he'd be getting.*

True, all true. But equally true that though confession might ease her conscience, it would inflict nothing but pain and humiliation on Jeremy. What right had she to do that?

Get off the pot, Annabel, the voice of conscience yawned, bored stiff with all this shilly-shallying about. *Either take charge of your life, or continue to be led around by the nose, and stop your whining.*

Take charge how, when time was rushing her along in a tide of events so fast-moving she had no control over them any longer?

Two more houseguests had arrived that morning, with more expected any time. Tomorrow, the caterers were coming to begin the job of erecting a huge tent on the back lawn, and a security firm was sending out two of its people to supervise the displaying of all those wedding gifts, stacked reproachfully in the downstairs den.

On Friday, her bridal outfit was to be delivered—the new one that she'd exchanged for the original, and that no one else knew about. The one Barbara Carson

147

had inspired her to choose the day the two of them had lunched together, and Annabel had decided she wanted to show the rest of the world that she knew how to be romantic and feminine as well as sensible and suitable.

And the day after that? That was her wedding day, which, unless she did something pretty quick, would also be the day she'd start to live the rest of her life on a lie.

Oh, she thought, sinking her head into her hands, it was too much for one person to deal with. She had never felt so alone in all her life. Her mother was besotted with Luke, and in any case had made it plain enough that if Annabel was hell-bent on going through with the wedding, she'd do it alone. Pandora was a child, not old enough to be burdened with such problems, and too involved in her new relationship with her father to realize how desperately her mother needed a little moral support.

And Luke? Oh, he had all the answers, except the one she most needed to hear. You're a nice woman to sleep with, Annie, though I'm not sure I'm up for marriage, but dump Jeremy, in case I change my mind.

"Pssst!" The whisper filtered through the room on a gust of air.

Oh great! Someone was at her door, probably Marion, checking to make sure the bride made it up the aisle with her virtue unsullied. If she only knew!

Hopping out of bed, Annabel opened her door a crack, but there was nothing to see but the glow of a lamp, and nothing to hear but the gentle snores coming from Marion's open door, across the hall.

No wonder she was hearing things, she thought, closing the door silently. She'd be seeing things next,

148

the state she was in. When she started catching invisible butterflies, they'd come in white coats and take her away. It couldn't happen soon enough.

"Psst, Annabel! Over here!"

Good grief, she was seeing things, too—a hand, groping around in the billowing drapes at her french doors, and right behind it, Luke's face, quickly followed by the rest of him. He wore nothing but a pair of cream linen pants, and she couldn't take her eyes off all that expanse of masculine chest, and those broad male shoulders. A more attractive rogue had never been created.

"Don't scream," he whispered. "I'm coming in."

Scream? The way her heart was palpitating, it was all she could do to draw breath.

"And don't faint," he warned her, alarmed, and covered the carpet between them to throw his arms around her.

"I wasn't planning to," she returned. He felt wonderful, smelled wonderful. "What are you doing here?" As if she cared! She was intoxicated by his audacity; light-headed with ridiculous happiness just to be held by him again.

The whole scene might have been something stolen from a comedy classic, she thought, smothering a sudden urge to laugh: the witching hour, a distraught bride, a secret lover hopping over the balcony, and the spinster aunt snoring across the hall. Hadn't Shakespeare written a play about this?

"You could've fooled me," Luke grumbled, peering into her face. "You're so pale, you look as if you've just been dug up."

Dug up? The words had her erupting into helpless giggles that went on and on until she was practically

149

squeaking. Surely Shakespeare hadn't come up with that immortal line! She wanted to tell Luke what it was she found so entertaining, but she couldn't stop giggling long enough to get the words out.

"Stop it!" he hissed, a smile playing over his mouth. "You'll wake up Fat, the Dragon Lady."

Well, that did it! The giggles multiplied and became even shriller, tripping out of her mouth like a waterfall. But he didn't look at all amused, suddenly. He looked quite severe instead, and she tried to sober up, covering her mouth with her hand, but it didn't help. In fact, she found herself cackling like an overwrought hen. It was a most unladylike sound, and she would no doubt be very embarrassed by it in the morning.

And then, he shook her. Really hard. Her head flew back and forth until she thought it would roll right off her neck, and she bit her tongue. She could taste the blood. It spoiled all the fun, and made her cry. The giggles stopped, and were replaced by big, fat tears that trickled down her face and onto his bare chest. She remembered, then, which play it was that she'd been reminded of. Not a comedy at all, but *Romeo and Juliet*, star-crossed lovers.

"I'm sorry," Luke muttered. "Darling Annabel, I'm so sorry, but you have to stop that noise and listen to me."

Well, she would if she could. She opened her mouth, intending to tell him so, and found herself saying something else entirely. "Oh," she sobbed, expelling the words on a sad little hiccup, "I have to tell you something, and I'm sorry if it upsets you, but I think I love you. Isn't that silly?" And she cried even harder.

"Oh, shit," he groaned, and crushed her to him and kissed her as if he thought she needed to be resuscitated. It was the most romantic moment of her life. His mouth covered hers so long and so desperately, and filled her with such warmth, that her toes curled up with delight, and eventually, even her tears dried up.

But he didn't stop kissing her. He walked her backward, until the pair of them toppled onto the bed, and he kissed her and kissed her as if he wanted to draw the very soul out of her. They were breathtaking kisses, as soft and deep as the dark pervading silence of a very black night, and Annabel wished she could as easily disappear into them, and never have to come back again.

"I want to talk to you," Luke told her in a low, gravelly voice that performed delicious miracles in her ear. "Stop attacking me this way."

"No," she begged, holding his face and turning his mouth back to hers. He'd had no business sneaking into her room, no business kissing her, but now that he'd started, she wasn't willing to end the magic. She may as well be hung for a sheep as a lamb. "No talking . . . not yet. Just love me . . . please . . ."

He ringed her hips with both hands in a parody of decorum. "Not now, darling Annabel," he whispered, willing his hormones to subside. Time enough for the loving when everything else had been resolved. But his eyes were teased by the glimpse of her breasts spilling out of her gown, and his skin impossibly aroused by the heavy satin that slithered against him in wanton invitation.

"Now . . . now," she heard herself beg, invaded by a recklessness most unsuited to her usual self. Nothing they might have to say to each other was more important than this. Her mind was too clouded with hunger to think logically, when she could feel him stirring against her, giving the lie to his refusal.

He released a sigh, defeat laced with desire, and let the passion run free, bold and unashamed and every bit as persistent as it had been eleven years ago. Who said a man was past his prime at forty? "You're a glutton for punishment, Annie," he murmured against her mouth, his hands sliding up to her breasts, and taking the satin nightgown with them.

But punishment was a double-edged sword, he discovered, as Annabel's elegant, clever hands tangled with the buckle at his waist, and tormented him with their lovely irreverence. Would there ever come a time, he wondered, when they could enjoy each other at leisure, and make love for the unhurried pleasure of it, without fear of discovery or consequences? "Ann-a-bel . . ." he sighed raggedly, as her fingers stole inside his pants and ran unhindered over him. And then he stopped thinking altogether and concentrated his energies and talents on reducing her to the same incoherent state of rapture to which she was subjecting him.

They needed to please one another, to give their love, their bodies, their hearts. Annabel continued stroking, fondling and kissing Luke until he thought he'd explode. But still he could not stop her. She moved on top of him and welcomed his hardness inside her.

As she rode him, her beautiful breasts teased his lips until he reached up and caught one in his mouth. He sucked and tasted and nibbled, and Annabel rode faster and faster, murmuring love words in his ear. Their loving took hold of them. They were spinning, flying, reaching the stars, and before he exploded in ecstasy, Luke grasped her buttocks and held her tightly to him, crying out his love.

Annabel was one with him, her ecstasy matching his, her body again responding in ways she never thought possible.

Their coming together was a celebration of love; candid and untouched by fear or regret, or any of the emotions that had colored their every other exchange. Their bodies, at least, recognized that the time for playing games was at an end, and that if there could not be uncomplicated honesty here and now, then there was no gaining it ever. In the pale light of the star-washed night, they discovered an affinity that ran deeper than the meshing of limbs, more complex than the union of man and woman; something spiritual and timeless and powerful.

"I love you, my Annabel," he told her, with quiet, irrevocable conviction. He had loved her from the very beginning, he now knew, but like a wine too young to be enjoyed, he had stored it in the recesses of his heart and almost forgotten about it. Until the last week, when he'd brought it out again and examined it, and found it seasoned and mature, and ready to be shared.

At his words, a gladness swelled up inside her until she thought her heart would burst. "Do you?" she whispered, the stars in her eyes rivaling anything the sky outside could conjure up. "Do you? Really?"

"Really."

"Oh, I love you, too." She buried her face against his chest, heard the steadfast beat of his heart, and believed she'd found the one haven she'd been searching for from the day she'd first met him. "What are we going to do about it?"

153

"I'm not about to do anything," he said, knowing he turned all the shimmering wonder in her to cruel shards of despair. He turned away from the stricken enormity of her eyes, and steeled himself to deliver the toughest blow he'd ever inflict on her. "What *can* I do?"

"Marry me," she gasped, recoiling from the shelter of his arms as though he'd struck her.

"Now how can I do that," he asked reasonably, "when you're marrying Jeremy, the day after tomorrow?"

"Not if you marry me first," she protested, her pride eclipsed in the dawning realization that it was Thursday already. "Please, Luke, let's run away . . . before it's too late."

No dice, Annie, he thought. You've got to want me badly enough to stand up before the whole world and say so. I'm not settling for a hole-and-corner elopement. "Leave Jeremy at the altar, you mean? Annabel, what's happened to your sense of social responsibility? Your sense of honor?"

"I don't have any," she wailed softly.

"Then you'd better find some."

"What about Pandora? We're her parents and she wants us to be together."

Luke thought of his conference with Pandora at the hot-air balloon show.

"I hope you've decided you can love me," she'd confided, her little face turned up to watch the balloons swooping down to land on the beach. "Because I've decided that I'd like to have you as my father, and I wouldn't mind everyone else knowing it, too."

"I would be honored," he'd told her. "Especially

154

since I've decided it would be impossible not to love you."

She'd given a little squeal, and hung on to his leg with glee. "Even if Mommy marries Jeremy?"

"Even then," he'd replied. "In fact, I'd thought that maybe we could stop by the Department of Vital Statistics on the way home. I would very much like to find out if we could have your birth certificate changed to show my name as well as your mother's. How would you feel about that?"

She had looked luminous in the sunshine. "Daddy," she said in her best grown-up voice, "I would feel very nice."

"And while we're there," he'd gone on, "there's another little task I have to complete. If I tell you about it, will you promise not to say a word to anyone, not even your grandmother?"

She'd crossed her heart and hoped to die if she so much as breathed a word.

"And you'll trust me, and not get scared at the last moment, no matter how bad things might look?" he'd concluded, after filling her in on his plans.

"You can count on me," she'd promised, delighted to be included in such an escapade. Then her face had clouded. "But are you sure it'll work?"

"No," he'd been forced to admit. "But I hope it will, and even if it doesn't, it won't make any difference to the way I feel about you."

Had he invested her with too much responsibility, he wondered now, Annabel's anguish gnawing at him. Would she be able to withstand seeing her mother pushed to such extremes, and not find her loyalties torn between them? Hang in there, Pandora, he

155

thought. We're into the home stretch, and coming up to the finish line.

"She doesn't have anything to do with this," he told Annabel cuttingly. "She and I have had some long talks, and we've straightened out where we stand with each other. I certainly don't need to elope with you in order to have a relationship with my daughter."

Darling, darling Annabel, he promised, seeing her face twist with pain, don't make me put you through this, please. "And after all," he concluded virtuously, "what would she think of me, sneaking you off like that? She expects me to act like a man."

"Then do so," Annabel practically screeched, at her wits' end. "Get me out of this mess!"

"Get yourself out," he snapped, and reached down to retrieve his clothes. "There's still time. You've got until tomorrow night, Annie, to get your act together, or I'll get my act on the road and save you the trouble!"

Then he hooked his thumbs inside his briefs, drew them up over his hips and, slinging his pants over one shoulder, left by the same route that he'd arrived.

Tomorrow night? Annabel sat in the middle of the bed and clutched the sheet under her chin, shivering as if it were the middle of December. Thirty-six hours before her wedding, and she had to stand up all by herself, and tell the world she was calling it off? Endure Jeremy's shock, his parents' outrage, Marion's scandalized twitterings? And all of it without a single, sympathetic soul by her side? Because she knew full well how her mother and daughter would receive the news. It would be all they could do not to clap their

156

hands with glee. They'd made plain how they felt the day they'd sent for Luke.

Oh, God, Annabel prayed earnestly, please give me the decency and the courage to do what I have to do—before tomorrow night.

CHAPTER TEN

Annabel arranged to meet Jeremy in the park near the hospital after her classes were over the next day. Jeremy was quite late, which wasn't like him, and she spent the time rehearsing a dozen ways of telling him, kindly, that she didn't think she could go through with the wedding. By the time he showed up, she was fit to be tied, because no matter how she phrased it, nothing altered the fact that he was being given the last-minute boot for another man. She didn't see how she could possibly make her own behavior seem excusable, when she knew he never would have treated her so shabbily.

"Sorry I'm late," he announced breathlessly, flinging himself down on the bench next to her. "I had a million things to take care of before going away."

"Going away?" she echoed, preoccupied with the opening lines of her own dialogue. Which would sound better: I'm not good enough for you, Jeremy; or, You don't really love me, so I think I should let you go?

He took her hand lightly in his. "On our honeymoon." He laughed. "Don't tell me you're such a bundle of nerves, you've forgotten about it?"

"Actually," she began, her voice sounding high and

unnatural, "that's one of the things I wanted to talk about."

"You've got enough on your mind," he told her, little knowing how true the words were, "without worrying about that. Leave it to me. Everything's taken care of."

If only Luke could be persuaded to act that way! "Um . . . well . . . I'm not sure . . . um . . . I mean, what if I don't . . . sort of go?" She felt her face flame, but the rest of her began to shake.

"Are you cold, Annabel?" he asked, strangely obtuse, she thought, for a man normally so perceptive. "It's a lovely afternoon—must be about eighty in the sun. I hope you're not coming down with something."

She shot him an agonized look. He was busy watching a squirrel running along the branch of a tree, more relaxed than she'd ever seen him. He'd stuffed his tie in his pocket, and was sprawled out at his ease, while she perched next to him as if she were sitting on hot coals. "Jeremy," she said in quiet desperation, "I'm not sure we should get married."

He continued to watch the squirrel. "Really?" he replied calmly. "Why not?"

"Because . . . because . . . of certain . . . things. Um, because I'm not sure my feelings are . . . right."

"Ah." He turned to her then, with that direct, observant gaze that allowed for no evasion. "So we're getting around to talking straight at last, are we?"

She felt shock drain the blood from her face. "At last? What 'y you mean?"

"I wondered how long you could go on like this, Annabel. Would you like to tell me, now, about Luke?"

"How did you know? How could you tell . . . ?" Her throat closed on the words, and she trailed into silence, at a loss to cope with anything but the overwhelming shame to which his question had given rise.

"My dear Annabel," Jeremy replied, and took her hand more firmly in his, "give me credit for some redeeming qualities, please. I'm neither blind nor insensitive, especially not where your happiness is concerned. I knew from the day he arrived here that Luke was your first love. What I hadn't realized until very recently is that he's also your last, and only, love."

Dismay had her uttering the first thing that came to mind. "Why didn't you tell *me*, then?"

For a moment, he seemed genuinely amused. "I thought it was something you had to learn about firsthand."

"You must hate me. How can you sit here with me, and be so civilized?"

Once more, he trapped her in that candid gaze. "I could never hate you, Annabel. In fact, I owe you something. I've learned a thing or two, as well, as a result of all this. You should see yourself when you look at Luke—all lit up inside. It's beautiful to watch, but it's made me realize how lacking our relationship is. I want a wife who looks at me the way you look at him—someone who sees her Prince Charming, and not just a surgeon who'll make a good husband." He laughed again, deprecatingly. "I may be a thirty-six-year-old fool, but I want to be obsessed by someone—not able to sleep or eat properly when I'm away from her, and know she's feeling the same way about me. Am I going through an early midlife crisis, do you think?"

Annabel gave a little groan of pure misery. He was trying hard to cover up, but his revelations gave her new insight into him. She had always seen him as a man of contained emotions. Not volatile, like Luke, but disciplined and sparing. A man of great kindness and generosity of heart, but detached—perhaps because that was the only way a surgeon survived the traumas he faced each working day. "I didn't think you needed that sort of love," she said, bewildered and appalled at her lack of insight.

"You weren't alone; I didn't either. In a way, we're both to blame, for being so ready to settle for second best. Put it down to ignorance, if you like, and thank your lucky stars Luke showed up in time to save you from making a mistake."

"How will we tell everyone? What reasons will we give?"

"We don't have to give reasons, Annabel. It's enough to say we've decided to cancel the wedding."

His strength and support should have been a comfort. But instead of relief, she felt terribly afraid. He was the most stable influence in her life; the most unselfish person she knew. Luke had left her to make her decision alone, but Jeremy was there, at her side, taking his share of the load. Was she making a dreadful mistake? What if all this uproar was nothing more than a bad attack of wedding nerves? What if, next week, or next month, she found she'd given up the best thing she'd ever known?

"I thought I'd feel better with everything sorted out between us," she said miserably, "but I don't. I feel so uncertain. Why can't things be black and white, instead of so gray?"

"They seldom are," he remarked, stroking her hand. "You have to be prepared to take a few chances, love, if you want to get the most out of life."

He called her "love" and meant it, she knew. Luke

called her "darling" and "sweet face," and she never knew whether he was being snide or not. "It's not that I don't love you," she tried to explain. "I do, and I can't imagine not having you in my life." The very thought that he wouldn't be there for her to lean on left her desolate. She started to cry in a quiet, hopeless kind of way.

"I love you too, Annabel, but I've never really let myself love you the way I know I could. Maybe I've known all along that you weren't as committed to me as you should have been. I think we all try, at some level, to protect ourselves from hurt, and perhaps this was my way."

But how much did Luke love her? she wondered, mopping at her tears without making the slightest impression on their flow. He made demands on her that taxed her to the limits of her endurance, and left her with nothing but the memory of his seduction to sustain her. "I'm frightened," she told Jeremy, knowing she could make the admission without incurring his scorn. "I don't know if I'm making the right decision. Tell me what I should do."

"You're the only one who knows where your heart really lies, Annabel."

He was kind and gentle, but he was a surgeon most of all, and whether he knew it or not, he did see things in terms of clear choices. He would not help her in this instance.

"You know yourself better than I know me," she suggested hopefully. "You call off the wedding." She could live with his rejection more easily than she could leave him. People talked about the pain of loving too much, but no one ever mentioned the grief that came from loving not quite enough.

"I couldn't do that, Annabel," he said with quiet finality. "I'd do a lot for you, but I won't let you put the responsibility for your life on my shoulders. It's time you took charge of your own destiny. If you want Luke, you'll have to give me up. It's as simple as that."

"It's not simple at all," she cried. "It's horribly complicated and messy. I can't do it by myself. I need you."

He touched her. Not earth-shatteringly or tenderly, as Luke did, but consolingly and kindly. Why couldn't she be satisfied with this, instead of wanting the best of both worlds? "You're too overwrought to make any decisions in your present state," he said. "Let me take you home so you can get some rest. Tomorrow is soon enough for you to decide how you want to handle this."

"Tomorrow's Friday. We can't afford to wait."

"When we're talking about the rest of your life, we have no other choice. We can't afford not to take time."

"Please stay with me. Don't leave me alone."

"I must. I have an appointment that can't be canceled, but I'll talk to you first thing tomorrow."

Luke had a bad case of heartburn, brought on by an equally bad case of nervous tension. He had earned some strange looks from the bartender by the time Jeremy joined him in the booth at the back of the bar. It was past eight, and the cocktail crowd had pretty well dispersed, so they had the place almost to themselves. "Well?" he demanded, "did she do it?"

Jeremy signaled the waiter. "I'm going to order a drink," he said. "What about you?"

Luke waved the offer aside in an agony of impatience. "What happened?"

The waiter stopped at their table. "Double Scotch, twice," Jeremy decided, then cast Luke a sardonic look. "How did I manage to wind up in the middle of this mess?" he inquired with amused irony. "I'm engaged to a pretty fantastic woman and I'm trying to palm her off on you. A lot of men would tell me I'm not playing with a full deck."

"You're not in love with her," Luke answered.

"It wouldn't take a lot to make me change my mind." Jeremy shot him an oblique glance. "She's in bad shape, you know. Are you sure we're going about this the best way?"

"You just answered your own question," Luke flung back. "What do you think? It's tough facing up to feelings when you've spent years ignoring them, but she has to take a stand, and neither you nor I can do it for her."

The waiter arrived with their drinks and a dish of shelled almonds. Jeremy raised his glass. "May the best man win, then."

Luke, about to join him in the toast, abruptly lowered his glass to the table. "Don't tell me you've changed your mind? I thought we understood each other."

"We do." Jeremy sipped his Scotch and shrugged. "Let me enjoy a few regrets, okay? With a bit of luck, it might have worked out for Annabel and me." He looked at Luke and grinned suddenly. "But it didn't, and unless I miss my mark, you'll wind up the winner."

"She agreed to call off the wedding?"

"She's a woman of conscience, Luke. A woman of integrity. She'll—"

"Never mind extolling her virtues to me, I've already enumerated them. Did she call it off?"

"Not quite. I gave her until tomorrow."

Damn! This was really cutting things close. "Couldn't you have—?"

"She's on the edge of nervous collapse. I'd prefer to see her ride off into the sunset with you in something other than an ambulance. We've come this far. What's a few more hours?"

An eternity, for Christ's sake! She wasn't the only one near the end of her rope.

"Hey!" Jeremy nudged him with his foot. "We more or less expected this, right? If I'd hung around and really pressed her, she'd probably have made the break tonight, but I knew you were waiting here, panting to hear how things were going, so I took her home and put her to bed."

"What!"

"Purely professional, I assure you. And I think it might be a good idea if we both make ourselves scarce tomorrow, until she's made up her mind. We have to give her every chance to make this decision on her own, and she's not going to find that easy with us breathing down her neck. Time's on our side for a little longer. The wedding's not until two o'clock on Saturday."

Annabel awoke after ten on Friday morning, staggered to find she could sleep so long when so much was hanging over her head.

"It's done you a world of good," Sybil told her, pouring her a cup of hot mocha chocolate, and carrying it out to the terrace for her. Annabel immediately felt very uneasy. Hot chocolate was her mother's cure-

165

all for every ailment under the sun. Why did she feel the need to offer it today?

"Has Jeremy called?" Annabel asked. "He said he would."

"No, dear heart." Sybil opened the sun umbrella over the table, and took a seat across from her daughter. "Isn't it a beautiful day?"

"Lovely, Mother. Where's Pandora?"

Sybil looked vague—another unsettling sign. Something was in the air, Annabel just knew. As if she didn't have enough to handle, without her family keeping secrets from her.

"Mother?"

"Annabel?"

"Where's Pandora?"

"Oh, she's around and about. Don't worry about her. Drink your chocolate, darling, before it gets cold."

Like my hands, Annabel thought, the skin on the back of her neck beginning to prickle. The house was extremely quiet, considering it was bulging at the seams with houseguests. "Where's Luke?"

"Luke?"

At Sybil's vacant expression, Annabel's hair took on a life of its own and stood out from her scalp. They were playing a game of cat and mouse here, and she was the mouse. "Yes, Mother, Luke. You surely haven't forgotten him, considering the lengths to which you went to bring him here?"

Sybil fiddled with her cup. "He's not here," she said.

"Oh? Where is he?"

There was another interminable pause. "He's gone."

"What do you mean, gone?"

"He packed his bags and left this morning, darling."

"Get your act together by tomorrow night, Annie, or I'll get mine on the road and save you the trouble." Annabel's hand started to shake so badly, the chocolate splashed out of the cup all over the table.

"Oh, darling child!" Sybil pushed back her chair so rapidly, it fell over backward. "What can I do?"

He said he loved me, Annabel thought bleakly, but he couldn't even wait until this morning for me to tell him I was going to do things his way. "Nothing, Mother."

She got up from the table and walked to the edge of the terrace on legs that felt like rubber. Summer had returned with a vengeance. The sky was clear, melting into the blue of the ocean without so much as a wisp of cloud to mar its perfection. Below, on the lawn that led to the beach, the catering crew was in the final stages of erecting a huge yellow and white striped tent. Tomorrow was her wedding day. Like the day a woman gives birth to her first child, it should have marked the beginning of a new era, full of happiness and anticipation. But now, as then, she'd allowed herself to fall under Luke's spell, and once again, he'd robbed the occasion of all its joy, then left her bewildered and heartbroken.

"Annabel," Sybil said at her side, "it isn't too late—"

"It's much too late, Mother." She couldn't even cry this morning; some things cut too deep to be so easily alleviated. She felt detached from everything around her, as though she were dead, but her body didn't know it yet. How could he do this, if he really loved her?

167

How long did you expect him to hang around? her little voice wanted to know. *Until you were at the altar?*

The sound of the doorbell filtered through the house to the terrace, and hung in a dying echo on the still summer air. It stirred the ashes in Annabel's heart, overriding the dictates of reason. "I'll get it," she told her mother, the words rippling out on a gust of hope. Perhaps he'd come back; perhaps he hadn't really abandoned her a second time.

She flew to the front door and wrenched it open, the accelerated rush of her heart a hurting clamor in her breast that soon thudded to a halt. It was not he. He would not come back, and make things easy for her. She'd left it too late.

"Ms. Pryce?" The two women on the doorstep were laden with boxes, the expressions on their faces as pleased as if they'd just been appointed Santa's little summertime helpers. "We're delivering your wedding outfit. Where would you like us to hang everything?"

"I'll show you." Sybil was at Annabel's shoulder, anxious to spare her daughter as much as possible. But it was beyond anyone's powers to halt time, and from then on, there was a stream of visitors arriving at the door, everyone with a task to perform that would guarantee a beautiful wedding day for the bride.

"Oh, Annabel, get the door, will you?" Sybil, trying to supervise the influx of strangers in her home, was caught between the doorbell and the phone, more flustered than Annabel had ever seen her. All that famous poise, that commanding sense of presence had evaporated, as arrangements made months earlier shifted smoothly into gear, impervious to the distress of the bride, the hovering anxiety of the bride's nother, or the escalating excitement of Pandora, who opped around the house like an agitated elf.

It was another delivery, this time from a downtown hop that specialized in imported crystal. Another be-ibboned gift to add to the stack in the den. Wearily, Annabel waved the man in the right direction. A mi-raine threatened, nagging behind her eyes. "In here," she said, and saw with relief that her mother was off the phone. "Who was it?" she asked, without much hope or interest. Luke was hardly likely to call to ay good-bye, and Jeremy would surely come in per-on to hear her decision.

"Er . . . the plumber," Sybil replied. "Young man, e sure you don't lose the card attached to that gift, or we won't know who sent it. Dear heart, you look like armed-over sin. Why don't you go and lie down for alf an hour before dinner?"

Annabel wondered what it was the plumber had said o restore her mother to her usual form with such apidity, but then decided she didn't care. Marion was oming in the front door, her heavily lacquered hairdo ainstakingly arranged, and Annabel seized on Sybil's uggestion with the closest thing to enthusiasm she'd hown all day. Anything to escape from this madhouse f activity. There was absolutely nothing she could do, xcept watch the clock tick closer and closer to tomor-ow.

eremy came to her that evening. He found her sitting y herself on the terrace, while inside the house, her other entertained the guests.

He leaned against the table, and looked at her long nd seriously. "It doesn't seem to me," he said at last, that you've done anything at all to indicate to your

169

mother that the wedding is off. In fact, I'd say, fro
the look of things, that we still have a date at the altar

"I've been sitting here, watching the stars com
out," she told him, "and thinking how unimportant w
are, how insignificant our problems are, in the great
scheme of things. Do you realize, Jeremy, that w
could both be dead, a week, a year, from now?"

"Melancholy thoughts, Annabel," he replied. "Do
that mean you've reached a decision?"

"We all need someone," she went on, as if he hadn
spoken. It was very important that she make him u
derstand exactly what she was saying. "Someone w
can count on, to be there when things get roug
someone who'll share the bad times, as well as t
good. Not to be alone is, I think, the greatest need w
have—that, and knowing that the other person is the
from choice, and not by accident of birth, like a pare
or child. And that's made me think about us, abo
what we shared until recently, and about what w
could still make of it, if we tried."

She dared to look at him then, and found hi
closely attentive. "What I'm trying to say," she co
cluded, before she lost her nerve, "is that we've con
too far and too close to throw it all away. We've nev
understood one another better. I'd like to try to be t
sort of wife I now know you want—but I'll understa
if you feel that's no longer possible."

"What about Luke?"

An inevitable question, and one she'd been expec
ing, but she still wished he hadn't asked, because the
was no time, any longer, for prevaricating. "Luke h
left," she told him. "And yes, that has everything to
with my request to you. If he had stayed, I wou
probably have canceled the wedding. But if he h

170

never come here in the first place, such a thing would never have occurred to me."

"But he did come, Annabel."

"And left again." She got up from her chair, and went to lean against him. "Jeremy, please let us go ahead with our wedding. Let's try to salvage something. Don't let him smash everything in my life, until all I have left are the ruins of my hopes and dreams."

He cradled her as if she were so fragile that she'd shatter with careless handling. "You love him," was all he said.

"I'm possessed by him. But you—you don't want my soul. You won't destroy me."

"I'm safe," he said.

"You give me security," she insisted, and wished with all her heart that the paucity of what she could offer him was not so glaringly apparent. But if he would rescue her this one time, she would spend the rest of her life making it up to him.

He released her enough to tip her chin with his finger. "I told you yesterday, Annabel, that this had to be your decision. I haven't changed my mind. But I want you to think again about what you're asking. There's still time for you to change *your* mind."

From the open windows of the house, laughter rippled over the muted sound of conversation. It was like a rerun of the night Luke had come back: everyone but she sublimely ignorant of the minor tragedy being enacted on the terrace. How had her energy become so depleted since then, so that now she felt too old and weary to battle anyone, about anything? The line of least resistance had never seemed so desirable an option.

"I cannot," she confessed. "I don't have the sort of

171

courage that would allow me to stand up in front of everyone and say the wedding is off. You should have been here today, Jeremy, and seen the activity. The whole house was rocking with preparations. It was like being on an express train, racing toward a prearranged destination, with no stops on the way. Now all I want is to arrive and get it over with. To get away from here, and lie under a palm tree and vegetate with you."

She felt him shudder, whether with laughter or aversion, she couldn't tell. "Go to bed, love," he advised, leading her around the terrace to the door that led into the dining room. "Sneak upstairs and let me say your good nights for you. Try to sleep, and when you wake up tomorrow, think again about what you're doing."

He placed a kiss on her forehead, one on each closed eye, and lastly laid cool lips against her mouth. He didn't thank her, or tell her he was glad. He didn't tell her he loved her, or that he'd make sure she never regretted this decision. "Whatever you decide, Annabel," was all he said, "I'll be there to support you tomorrow."

It was the best he could offer her, and the best she had a right to expect.

CHAPTER ELEVEN

Annabel lay awake well into the dawn of her wedding day, listening to the murmur of waves on the shore and the quiet passing of the moon, her mind as empty as her heart. Not until the house began to stir did she fall asleep, and then it was suddenly and fathomlessly, like falling into a black hole. No dreams, no thrashing of limbs, but a repose as peaceful as death.

When she awoke, the sun was high, spilling over the bed and teasing her shoulders with warmth. She opened her eyes as Pandora came peeping around the door.

"Are you excited, Mommy?" she demanded, skipping around the bed.

That she should have to ask! Annabel felt sure her expression was more suited to a funeral than a wedding. "Excitement is for children, Pandora."

Her daughter looked at her with a compassion far beyond her years. "I hope I don't grow old like you," she pronounced. "It's no fun, is it?"

Annabel could have wept.

"Good morning, darling daughter!" The door swept open a second time, to admit Sybil, bearing a breakfast tray. "Was there ever a bride so beautiful!"

Annabel knew she looked like hell. And old. And miserable.

"How's our little bride?" Oh, God help her, Marion was in the room, too, hairdo swathed in a protective net bonnet that tied under her chins. "My dear, you should see the weather! It couldn't be better. If ever there was an auspicious sign! This is surely a marriage made in heaven."

Annabel looked at the croissants and coffee on her tray, and thought she might be ill.

"Eat, dear heart," her mother exhorted her. "We don't want you fainting at the altar."

Privately, Annabel thought that might be a very good idea. "I'm not hungry, Mother."

"Coffee, then?"

Not hot mocha chocolate, Annabel noticed. Apparently Sybil was convinced all was well with her first and last born. So much for maternal insight. "Please."

"Is that the dress?" Marion spared a glance for the tissue-draped hanger suspended from the door of the closet, before swooping on the croissants, and delving into the little pot of preserves next to them. "I hope Jeremy hasn't seen it. It's bad luck, you know."

"Mommy?" Pandora was posing before the mirror, turning her head this way and that. "I think I've changed my mind about curls for today. How d'you feel about gel? Like Cyndi Lauper?"

Sybil shuddered. "Perish the thought, child! Isn't she the one with hysterical hair? This is your mother's wedding day, not a circus."

That was debatable, Annabel thought, and wished they'd all leave, so that she could compose herself for the ceremonial rites that lay ahead. "Don't let me keep

174

you," she suggested. "I'm sure you've all got lots to do."

"This is your day," Marion scolded, croissant crumbs dangling from one of her chins. "Our little bride comes first."

Please God, Annabel prayed, give me the strength to get through this day without mortally insulting someone, and I'll never ask another unreasonable thing of you.

"Can I wear nail polish?" Pandora wanted to know.

"Yes." Anything; anything at all.

"Red?"

"No."

"You're no fun, Mommy."

"So you keep telling me." She swung her legs out of bed.

"The flowers have arrived, darling, and they're lovely. The freesias smell divine."

"And my dear nephew sent a corsage for me," Marion added fondly. "He knows how I adore orchids."

Annabel wondered uncharitably how Jeremy's aunt could find room to pin orchids on that imposing bosom, and still be able to see where she was going. Unseemly thoughts for a bride, indeed.

"It's almost eleven, Annabel," Sybil said. "Would you like me to fix Pandora's hair, so you can dress in peace?"

"I'm a bridesmaid," Pandora objected. "It's my job to help the bride."

"Perhaps later," her grandmother suggested. "I thought we'd have a light lunch, then we should all start to get ready. Guests will probably start arriving around one."

"No lunch for me, Mother. I'm going to run a bath,

and give myself a manicure." Keep busy until the last minute. Make herself as dazzling a bride as possible. It was the least Jeremy deserved. And leave herself no time to think; no time to search her scruples, and ask herself if she had the right to demand so much of Jeremy, when she had so little to offer him in exchange.

Sybil plopped a kiss on her cheek. "We'll be back," she whispered, indicating Pandora, then herded everyone out of the room.

So, dearie, her little voice began, the minute the door closed, *you're really going to put this nice man through all this hoopla, just to save your skinny neck? I'm ashamed to be sharing accommodation with such consuming selfishness.*

Annabel went through to her bathroom and turned on the hot water. I'm giving him the rest of my life, she argued, pouring crystals into the tub. I'll make a career out of this marriage. He'll be happy.

Conscience made a rude noise. *The only thing you know how to make a career out of is misery, and that's all he'll be getting if he marries you.*

Annabel lowered herself into the bath, sank down in the water till it lapped at her chin, and turned off her mind. There was silence, unbroken except for the twittering of birds in the trees outside the window. She almost relaxed.

Then the doorbell rang, and there came the sound of footsteps marching through the house, the sound of voices, the sound of efficiency at work. Time for her to get a move on, too.

You're not really a bad person, the little voice conceded, pityingly, *just stunned. Poor thing.*

Annabel turned on the shower, and shampooed her hair vigorously, then stepped out of the tub and wrapped herself in a towel. She dried her hair, and powdered and perfumed her body. She painted her toenails Japanese plum blossom pink, and tipped her fingers to match. Then she went to sit at her dressing table, so that she could achieve with cosmetics what her face lacked in the way of natural radiance and joy. The trouble began when she looked through the mirror at the room behind her, and saw the reflection of her bed. In a flash, she was transported back to that night over a week ago when she'd sat in the same place, in a similar state of undress, and found her eyes settling on Luke's feet.

At that, the numbness that had so mercifully enwrapped her since yesterday dissipated, and her heart filled with such an aching, grieving need, such a hopeless sense of loss, that the mascara wand slipped from her fingers and rolled among the jars and tubes spread out before her.

She had not known that there was such pain in all the world. Nor had she known it was possible for a heart to weather such an onslaught of torment and still continue to beat life into its body. Anguish washed over her, merciless and unending, until she felt physically ill, and had to lower her head between her knees, or faint.

She could have had it all with Luke, she realized. All the passion, and all the living that came from really loving. But in return for that, he'd demanded independence of her, had wanted a partner who'd share, not a parasite who fed on his strength. And she had dallied too long, savoring her insecurities and propping herself up on her contrived notions of acceptable courtship. He'd lost patience, and she'd lost him and the chance to experience a little bit of heaven here on earth. Because that sort of loving was too rare and wonderful a gift to be offered a second time. No amount of wishing would conjure it up between her and Jeremy. The magic was beyond them.

She couldn't bear to dwell on what she'd given up. Such squandering was impossible to forgive.

"Annabel! Dear heart, are you ill?" Sybil's hands cradled her hair, slid to test her brow, then brought her head to rest against her mother's shoulder.

"Mommy!" Pandora, Annabel noticed blearily, was gazing at her wide-eyed. "You can't get sick now. Those men have come and they're playing waiting music for the guests."

"Come along, darling." Sybil hauled her to her feet with surprising energy. "The best way to combat wedding nerves is action. Time to get dressed."

"Do you like my hair, Mommy? And my dress?" Pandora pirouetted around the room, endearingly conceited.

"You should see the cake, Annabel. It's a triumph."

"But it doesn't have a little bride and groom on the top," Pandora lamented.

"Praise the Lord!" Sybil breathed gratefully. "Which earrings are you planning to wear, my lamb?"

"I wish I could wear high heels like these. When can I, Mommy?"

"Annabel, my darling child, where did this incredible dress come from? It's nothing like the one you ordered in March. And this hat—dear heart, it's absolutely delicious!"

What was wrong with the pair of them? Annabel wondered in mute despair. How could the two people who knew her best be so entirely lacking in empathy or sensitivity, that they couldn't feel her misery? The inconsequence of their chatter was an affront, their pleasure in her clothing an insult. "Mother . . ."

Sybil took one look at her face. "Milk of magnesia for you," she declared with unaccustomed heartiness. "Pandora, go to my room, and look on the first shelf in the bathroom cabinet. The blue bottle—you know the one."

Pandora scurried off in a flurry of embroidered cotton and curls entwined with baby's breath.

"She looks like an angel, doesn't she?" her grandmother remarked fondly.

"Mother, there's something—"

"Into the pantyhose, darling." Sybil held up the lace concoction admiringly. My goodness, any finer, and they wouldn't be there."

"Mother, I'm trying to tell you—"

"Not on your life," Sybil muttered, folding the tissue paper that had covered the wedding dress with a great deal more ado than was necessary. "I'm getting you dressed and at the altar on time, if it kills both of us."

"What did you say, Mother?"

Pandora came back into the room. "Pills for both of us!" Sybil proclaimed, seizing on the bottle her granddaughter clutched in her hand. "Good old reliable milk of magnesia pills. They've saved the day for many a bride." She popped one in her mouth, shook two more into Annabel's limp palm and thrust the glass of water Pandora brought in from the bathroom into the other.

Annabel glared mutinously at her family, lips firmly pressed together. For heaven's sake, they'd both been so anxious to tell her, each in her own inimitable fashion, that she was a fool to marry Jeremy. But now, when she was trying to tell them they'd been right, they didn't want to hear it. It was one thing, she thought bitterly, for them to criticize, to offer unsolicited advice, and something else, suddenly, to be held accountable for her acting on it.

"Come along, Annabel," Sybil warned. "Open, close and swallow, or else."

"Moth—" Beset on all sides, Annabel made the tactical error of opening her mouth to voice her protest, and Sybil, mistress supreme of opportunity, took unhesitating advantage.

"That's a girl! Wonderful! Don't you feel better already? Take the glass, Pandora. On your feet, Annabel. Time to step into this gorgeous confection."

Very well, Annabel decided, we'll continue with the charade a little longer. The silk whispered over her skin, clung around her waist and swooped elegantly from one shoulder to the other.

"Oh, Mommy," Pandora breathed, nimble fingers anchoring the tiny pearls of buttons into place, "you look pretty."

The words produced a little thaw inside Annabel that gave her fresh courage. "Has Jeremy arrived?" Perhaps she could see him alone, before things went much further.

"An hour ago, at least. He's down in the garden, sitting in the front row with his parents. Don't keep him waiting any longer, darling. It's almost two o'clock."

"Here's your hat, Mommy. Shall we help you with it?"

"Better she does it herself," Sybil said, her voice all smoky and tender. "She knows just how she wants it to sit."

Annabel stood in front of the mirror, and lifted her arms, the sheer sleeves of her gown belling gracefully from her wrists to her elbows. "Like this, do you think?" She angled the wide lace brim to one side.

"Almost." Sybil's voice was a whisper. "Tilt it a little, dear heart, over one eye. It makes you look shy and demure, the way a bride should."

There was a tap at the door.

"I'm looking for a bride to give away," Annabel's godfather announced, "and I've got my hands full of flowers. Is someone going to let me in?"

"Get the door, Pandora," Sybil commanded, then turned to her daughter. "Come and see yourself in the full-length mirror, my darling. You're a vision."

Oh my goodness, Annabel thought, not quite believing what she saw. It wasn't her own reflection that held her attention, but her mother's. Sybil, superbly elegant, impeccably tasteful in dusky rose, stood beside her. And her indomitable mother, who refused to yield an inch to man or God, was crying—with style, of course, but crying, nonetheless. It was enough to make Annabel weep for what she knew she must do to her.

The music gathered importance, the guests stood and turned to watch, and ahead of her, Pandora stepped the length of the roll of white carpet with rehearsed precision, reveling in her moment of glory. Spying Jeremy at the flower-covered dais, Annabel trembled briefly, and wished bravery could have made its presence felt sooner. Jake gave her hand a paternal squeeze. "Here we go, sweetheart."

Except for the faces following her, approving, curious, affectionate, it might have been the last mile to

181

the gallows. Marion peering around her orchids, bosom heaving with excitement; Barbara Carson, appropriately dewy-eyed, and Dr. Carson, solemn and proud. Reverend Paton, who'd christened her, beaming benignly. Her mother, looking at her watch, for God's sake! And Jeremy, inscrutable, unsmiling.

Her gaze locked with his.

"Please be seated," the minister invited the guests, and spread his hands, encompassing the entire assembly. "We are gathered here," he began.

Annabel drew a deep breath, and ushered up the tattered remnants of her fortitude. "Excuse me, Reverend Paton."

He stopped abruptly. "Annabel?"

She gulped and almost lost her nerve. "I'm so sorry," she muttered, plowing on hurriedly, "but I'm afraid there isn't going to be a wedding. Not today."

"Are you sure, Annabel?" Jeremy took her hand, not protestingly, but supportively. From the front row, Annabel heard his mother give a faint gasp of incredulous dismay.

"I'm not even going to ask you to forgive me," Annabel told him, "for embarrassing you like this, in front of our families and friends, but by the time I knew I had the courage to release you, it was too late to stop . . . all this." She gestured helplessly at all the protocol of the wedding into which she'd thrust him.

He nodded understandingly, her beloved friend. "You may not have known, but I never doubted you for a minute."

"I wish I could give you good reasons for having asked you, yesterday, to submit to all this—settling for so much less than you deserve or need, just so I could

182

save face. I didn't know I could be so selfish. I think it's only in the last week that I've begun to know myself at all."

Behind them, the guests rustled, not able to hear, but knowing that all was not proceeding according to plan. The faintest hum of inquiry rose from their well-bred mouths.

Jeremy bestowed his warm, handsome smile on her. "I'd call it rediscovering yourself. Do you like what you see?"

She lifted her shoulders in a little shrug of disgust. "No. How could I? I see a taker and a coward."

You'd have seen them a lot sooner, if you'd listened to me, her little voice intoned virtuously.

"Mom-meeee!" To Annabel's left, Pandora let out an ear-splitting squeal of pure glee. "Look!"

The hum from the guests rose to a buzz that broke quickly into outright commotion. Jeremy looked at Sybil, who was smiling and indicating something out to sea, then raised startled eyes in the same direction. "You have company, love," he said, and turned Annabel around to face the congregation.

No one was looking at them. They'd lost all interest in her little drama. They were facing the other way, their eyes glued to the sight of the huge balloon that was drifting slowly to the beach. It settled on the sand, its scarlet and orange parachute swaying in tune to the breeze, puffed up with staccato blasts of hot air. And clambering over the side of the gondola was the man who'd wrought the most cataclysmic disorder in Annabel's heart, and brought her finally to this moment of self-awareness and strength.

"Daddy! Daddy!" Pandora hopped up and down like one possessed. Two rows back, Marion let out a shriek, and across the aisle from the Carsons, Sybil checked her watch again and drew a visible sigh of relief. Annabel pressed a hand to her mouth to stifle the laughter and wonder and suspense that warred for escape. She felt on the brink of giddy hysteria.

He came sprinting across the beach and up the lawn, scattering guests in all directions. "My goddamned knees are killing me," he groaned to Jeremy when he reached the dais, then turned to Annabel and swept her into his arms.

For the second time in as many weeks, all hell broke loose among the guests. Annabel heard Marion's enraged squawk soar above the general hubbub, just before the pianist struck up the opening bars from "The Bartered Bride."

"If you've talked Jeremy into marrying you," Luke whispered in Annabel's ear, "I'll hang myself."

"I haven't," she told him, her eyes as deep as sapphires, and twice as luminous. "I just called the whole thing off."

"A balloon?" Jeremy—that contained and disciplined man she thought she knew so well—was practically in stitches. "Isn't there enough hot air around here without that?"

"The bridge is closed because of an accident," Luke explained. "Traffic's backed up halfway across town. I had to do something, or I'd never have made it on time. As it is, I've cut it pretty close."

"But a hot-air balloon! Is it legal?"

"Probably not," Luke admitted, then folded Annabel into a kiss that stole her breath away.

"Just a minute," she gasped, when he allowed her to surface for air, "there's something fishy going on here. How did you know I'd back out at the last minute?"

"I didn't," he told her, his eyes feasting on every inch of her. He was enchanted. She looked . . . ethereal, her skin warm as ivory against the pure, unsullied white of her gown, her waist as fragile as glass under the close-fitting satin. He had to touch her, to make sure she was real, and not another teasing dream. "Oh, my Annabel," he whispered, gathering her into his hands in fervent hunger, "I have been so afraid I'd lose you again. Only here . . . now . . . do all the empty years make sense. You were worth the gamble."

She looked around: at her mother, the Cheshire cat personified; at her daughter, bursting with secrets. "I'm the only one who's surprised," she exclaimed.

"I promised I wouldn't tell, didn't I?" Pandora chortled, her curls flying about in disarray.

"You were wonderful," her grandmother confirmed. "We're really proud of you."

Luke released that disarmingly wicked grin that never failed to devastate Annabel's senses, capturing Sybil and Pandora in its spell. "We make a great team, the three of us," he boasted.

"Four," Jeremy corrected him.

Annabel felt her mouth fall open, leaving her looking as much like the village idiot as she had the night Luke had first shown up at the house. "You were all in on this?"

"I wasn't," Marion piped up. "Did you hear what that child called this man?"

"Daddy," Pandora supplied, in case anyone had missed it, and Marion almost aspirated on her orchids.

Reverend Paton cleared his throat ominously. "Is there to be a wedding or not?" he inquired testily. "Other people want to get married today, even if you don't."

185

Luke trapped Annabel in his gaze. "Well, darling Annie, is there? The choice is yours."

She let her eyes love him. He was elegant in morning suit, a carnation in his lapel. Not perfect, and not always easy to live with, perhaps, but the man for her. "Oh yes," she breathed, a gladness permeating her heart that she had done what she had to do, unaided, before he came swooping down out of the sky.

"Do you have a license?" Reverend Paton inquired, containing his impatience with difficulty.

"Yes," Pandora informed him. "We got one the other day. Show him, Daddy."

Annabel marveled anew at the duplicity of her nearest and dearest.

"And a ring?"

"Ring? Pandora, how come we forgot that?"

"Oh, shee-oot, Daddy, I don't know."

"I have the ring," Jeremy declared. "I knew I'd be of some use before the day was out."

Annabel tried to lower her eyes. Luke was staring at her with such intent, his glasses were beginning to steam up. She allowed the brim of her big lace hat to dip down concealingly.

"Sweet face," Luke told her, tucking his glasses into his pocket and anchoring her firmly against him with one arm, "you look like the Flying Nun in that outfit. Don't tell me I went to the expense of renting a hot-air balloon to carry you off, all for nothing?"

Oh, he was the right man, all right. The best man The only man.

JAYNE CASTLE

excites and delights you with
tales of adventure and romance

____TRADING SECRETS

Sabrina had wanted only a casual vacation fling with the rugged Matt. But the extraordinary pull between them made that impossible. So did her growing relationship with his son—and her daring attempt to save the boy's life.
19053-3-15 $3.50

____DOUBLE DEALING

Jayne Castle sweeps you into the corporate world of multimillion dollar real estate schemes and the very private world of executive lovers. Mixing business with pleasure, they made *passion* their bottom line.
12121-3-18 $3.95